"These spare, unsentimental, and skillful stories draw us in from the start. Tim Tomlinson obliges us to confront our failures and foibles without flinching, writing with searing honesty and considerable courage about people in trouble of various kinds—and does that not include us all?"

—Sheila Kohler, author of *Once We Were Sisters*, a memoir, and the novels *Cracks*, *Dreaming for Freud*, and ten other works of fiction.

Winter Goose Publishing
45 Lafayette Road #114
North Hampton, NH 03862

www.wintergoosepublishing.com
Contact Information: info@wintergoosepublishing.com

This Is Not Happening to You

COPYRIGHT 2017 © by Tim Tomlinson

First Edition, October 2017

Cover Illustration: "What She Was Calling For," by Mari Otsu
Cover Design by Winter Goose Publishing
Typesetting by Odyssey Publishing

ISBN: 978-1-941058-72-5

Published in the United States of America

"*This Is Not Happening to You* ranges with imaginative ease across locales and characters—a wealthy socialite in the Hamptons, a bitter, old Korean War vet in the suburbs, a thirty-something New Orleans barfly with delusions of grandeur, and many others. Quickly sketched but fully realized, these figures stumble into extreme (yet somehow plausible) situations that expose their all-too-human delusions. Above all, Tomlinson focuses on the cruel and inventive ways that desire makes each of us in turn predator and prey, martyr and buffoon. In the hands of a less assured talent these stories would offer only a grim ledger of sin and stupidity, yet Tomlinson leavens them with humor that is by turns wry, searing, and tender, although never sentimental. Sui generis as Tomlinson's sensibility is, it draws on one of the richest traditions in American Letters, the New York state of mind. By turns sardonic, irreverent, bold, psychologically astute and always engaging, Tomlinson has placed himself in the company of celebrated New York writers past, a pantheon that includes Hart Crane, Anatole Broyard, Dorothy Parker, and above all, Leonard Michaels, who would have recognized a kindred spirit in the magician of TINHTY. While the Manhattan that inspired generations of artists has all but disappeared, in Tomlinson's stories we encounter a late florescence of a unique sensibility, 'Made in New York' stamped on every page."

—Robert Anasi, author of *The Gloves: A Boxing Chronicle*,
and *The Last Bohemia: Scenes from the Life
of Williamsburg, Brooklyn*

"*This Is Not Happening to You*, the debut collection of stories from New York writer Tim Tomlinson, might just rescue the twenty-first century literati set from a jetlag inducing conservatism and PC hysteria. Tomlinson gets to the gutsy and often hilarious truth of who we are in prose that's poetic and unforgiving—like a well-timed right hook. No sprigs of lavender here. Just a heady and sardonic car crash of characters you won't be able to turn away from: murderous movie star widows, wild boys and their dogs, rogues and their half-grasped lovers, people on all kinds of edges, ex-poets at the bar. Tomlinson has the audacity to tell it how it is and we should get down on our knees and thank some dank, dark force of nature for that."

—Sally Breen, author of *Atomic City*, a novel, and the memoir *The Casuals*

"If you like your short fiction sweet and prim with nice neat endings that land on the right side of the fuzzy moral line, DO NOT READ THIS BOOK. If you prefer your characters a bit unsavory, morally challenged, and wildly memorable, you will not be able to put down this kick-ass collection. With Zen-like mastery of language, a razor-sharp eye for detail, and talent for finding danger and surprise in the familiar, Tomlinson holds his own with the best writers of the genre."

—Bronwen Hruska, author of *Accelerated*

THIS IS NOT HAPPENING TO YOU

STORIES BY
TIM TOMLINSON

Winter Goose
PUBLISHING
where words take flight

For Deedle,
whose bright spirit helps me
escape these dark places

"Human beings make a strange fauna and flora. From a distance they appear negligible; close up they are apt to appear ugly and malicious. More than anything they need to be surrounded with sufficient space—space even more than time."

—Henry Miller, *Tropic of Cancer*

CONTENTS

Look Closer 1

Trap 9

Before and After Science 17

Paris 33

Blasphemy 35

Shadow 39

Græy Area 43

The Perfect Throw 53

The Motive for Metaphor 57

Tonight and Forever 63

Autumnal 73

Snow Job 87

Travel 117

The Paula and Cliff Fragments 137

This is Not Happening to You 141

Just Tell Me Who It Was 153

Reunion 161

What She was Calling For 167

Shanghai 175

Acknowledgements 179

About the Author 180

LOOK CLOSER

"I know you all know what a dick is," Rosie said to the sixth-grade girls. "Well, here's mine."

From the open zipper in his jeans, Rosie fished his little eraser of a penis.

Some of the girls gasped and covered their mouths with their hands. Some laughed. Some pretended to look away, but few actually could.

They were in the woods just off the recess field, their perimeter guarded by fourth and fifth grade boys.

Rosie said, "You can look closer if you want."

Kathy Christmas pulled the hair from her face and leaned closer. Maria Bella and Debbie Fancy followed.

Debbie said, "Is it . . . is it getting bigger?"

The soft little pink thing had lengthened, the wrinkles in its shaft smoothed and hardened.

"Probably," Rosie said. "It sometimes does that."

Kneeling now, looking more closely, Kathy Christmas said, "Weird."

Rosie said, "It's okay to touch it."

"I'm not touching that," Kathy said, laughing.

Maria Bella knelt alongside her. "I will," she said.

She placed the tip of her index finger on the shaft and the penis hardened further.

"Why is it doing that?" Maria asked.

Rosie said he didn't know.

Maria said, "It's so smooth."

Debby Fancy leaned forward. She put her finger on, too, right at the tip.

"Ewww," she said, "it's all gooey." But she didn't take her finger away.

Then Billy Kanes, a fourth grader, came racing through the scrub.

"Morawski," he shouted once, and vanished up the path.

Violently, the girls on the periphery scattered into the woods. They disappeared quickly up the paths through the low scrub. Before they could be identified, they would all find hidden exits onto the playing field. But Kathy and Maria were slow getting up from where they knelt. Soil stuck to the knees they exposed between mini-skirts and the tops of white go-go boots. And Rosie was having trouble pressing his erection back into his jeans.

Then Mrs. Morawski appeared.

"Do not a single one of you move," she said.

Rosie was a new kid. His mother married Chris Hulse's father, and they arrived in town from Nassau County some place close to the city. They lived at the edge of a sod field stadiums wide. You could see their house all the way from 25A. It looked like a red Monopoly hotel at the corner of a ping-pong table.

Rumors preceded Rosie's appearance in school. He'd been left back at least once—he should have been in the seventh grade, maybe even eighth. There may have been some trouble in his last school, something to do with Rosie in the shower after gym class. Chris Hulse told his friends he wouldn't sleep in the same room as Rosie, but he didn't fully explain why. He moved into the basement where he slept on the couch, and he acted like he preferred that, but there was more to the story.

No one, not even Rosie when he arrived, could explain why Rosie was called Rosie. His real name was John Scratchley. One thing Chris said: "My father better not adopt him. I don't want the same last name as that fat freak."

Rosie wasn't really fat, he was chubby. He wore size 32" jeans, and his freckled face was puffy at the cheeks and under the chin. His hair was very short, a crew cut, the kind boys got when they got into trouble, but you could see that it was blond.

In the office, Kathy and Maria and Rosie stood, hands folded, in front of Principal Siegel's desk. Principal Siegel was new, too, but not as new as Rosie. He was supposed to be strict, but all he did now was look from Kathy's face to Maria's to Rosie's and back again. He drummed the fingers of one hand on his desk and continued to watch their faces. You could hear a watch tick, and sounds from the hall filtered in like echoes in a tunnel.

Finally, Kathy said, "Are we gonna just, like, stand here?"

Rosie snorted, and Maria bit hard on her lower lip.

"I mean," Kathy said, "we're missing I think social studies or some crap."

The three of them, then, led by Rosie, burst out laughing. They laughed against their efforts to hold in the laughter. Tears leaked from their eyes onto the floor of Principal Siegel's office where they splotched and darkened the gray and white tiles. They tried to suck back their guffaws, they tried to straighten from their waists, but they couldn't. It seemed almost like the harder they tried to stop, the more the laughter poured forth. But slowly, painfully, they gulped it back, they swallowed it down, until they mastered it and they all three stared at the floor and avoided each other's moist reddened eyes.

Principal Siegel continued drumming his fingers, for a minute, another minute, an eternity.

Kathy said, "Dude," and their laughter exploded again.

Rosie said, "I'm gonna piss my fucking pants," and they laughed harder and harder, their stomachs twisting into knots, and they pleaded with each other to stop, but they couldn't, again, for a very long time.

When they looked up this time, Principal Siegel was reaching for the phone.

Maria Bella's mother arrived second.

"He just showed it to us, Mama," Maria said, ducking blows. "How were we supposed to know?"

To Rosie's mother, Mrs. Bella said, "I'm gonna have that freak of yours locked up, you hear me?"

Mrs. Hulse stood behind Rosie holding his shoulders, sniffling back tears.

"We're both sorry," she told Mrs. Bella.

Mrs. Bella pushed Maria out the door. "Sorry my ass," she said over her shoulder. "You can tell it to the judge."

Kathy Christmas's mother wasn't home. Kathy was sent to spend the rest of the day in the nurse's office.

"What were you thinking," Nurse Meadows asked her.

"I dunno," Kathy said. "Just how funny and little it looked."

Nurse Meadows was taken aback. She fixed the glasses hanging round her neck onto the bridge of her nose.

"Funny and little," she repeated. "Young lady, do you have any idea what you have done?"

"Yeah," Kathy said, "I, like, looked at a dick. What's the big deal?"

Nurse Bellows sent Kathy back to Principal Siegel's office,

but on the way she ducked into the unfinished wing of the new school. She entered an empty classroom whose unlocked doors opened onto a staircase to the side drive. She flashed across the drive faster than a squirrel, and back home she ignored the ringing telephone and watched cartoons.

When she got bored, she went outside and walked through the woods to Maria Bella's house on John Street. She tapped at Maria's window.

"My mother's gonna kill me," Maria said, pulling her friend over the sill.

"Fuck your mother," Kathy said.

Kathy was something of a leader. Of all the girls, she developed noticeable breasts first, early in the fifth grade. By early sixth, which she was in now, she'd hung out with seventh and eighth grade boys, and she'd been felt up seven times. Maria had been felt up once. Debby Fancy wanted to be, but Kathy told her she needed to wait until there was something to feel.

"What did it feel like," Kathy asked, "when you, like, touched it."

"I don't know," Maria said, "kind of soft and smooth like velour."

Kathy said, "Really?"

"Even when it got hard," Maria said.

Kathy said, "Wow."

Maria said, "I know."

"But it didn't feel gooey? Debby said it was gooey."

"It didn't feel gooey to me."

Kathy said, "You think we should call her?"

"I can't call anyone," Maria said. "My mother would kill me."

"How would she know."

"That bitch knows everything."

"You should come to my house," Kathy said. "My mother lets us alone."

Maria said, "Yeah, well my mother loves me."

"What's that supposed to mean?"

"Just she loves me, that's all."

"And what, my mother doesn't?"

From another part of the house, Maria's mother shouted.

"What's all that noise in there?"

Maria said, "You better get out of here."

Kathy said, "You're such a wuss."

Maria said, "Okay, I'm a wuss. But I know more than you."

Kathy took the other woods, the woods that led away from home. She felt unsettled. She felt something had changed. She was the leader, the first one with a bra, the first one with a boyfriend, the first one French kissed, the first one felt up. It was like a shelf full of trophies. Then, all of a sudden, one shitty recess, and she's the one asking questions. What the hell did Debby mean, all gooey?

Rosie stood in front of the mirror looking at the way his little dick must have looked when he pulled it out. He thought about how it had lengthened and how good that felt, like something really good was about to happen. *Had* to happen. And he thought about how much fun it was in Principal Siegel's office, to laugh right in his face. No matter how much trouble he was in, it was worth it finally to laugh right in one of their faces.

He was in a lot of trouble, he knew that. He didn't know exactly how much, but the phone had been ringing nearly non-stop since the school buses dropped the kids back home. He could hear his mother crying, sighing, apologizing. And once his step-brother came in, without knocking, and said, "Dad's gonna send you to a home."

"*This* is my home," Rosie told him.

His brother said, "This is *our* home, you fat freak," and he slammed the door.

Rosie liked Chris. He was a fast runner, good at math, but he was so uptight.

In the mirror, he could see the distant traffic rolling on 25A. It was almost thirty minutes to the nearest town, a town with a luncheonette and a pharmacy and a candy store. He felt like he was living nowhere, at the edge of a huge lawn that didn't even have houses.

The school buses were just heading back out to pick up the late kids, the kids who stayed after for sports or clubs. Rosie had wanted to join a club. He thought he could do cross-country, but his step-brother told him they don't accept fat freaks. Then he thought he could do quilting, but Mrs. Morawski told him that was only for girls.

Something in the mirror caught his eye. He went to the window, and there . . . halfway across the sod field . . . was a figure . . . a girl . . . in a skirt . . . a mini-skirt . . . and white go-go boots . . . Kathy . . . Kathy Christmas. And she was coming toward his house. She was coming closer. And closer. So close she saw him. She saw him and waved. She indicated with her hands that he should lift up his window.

He looked down. He was still unzipped.

He wondered if he should raise his zipper. He guessed Kathy could tell him.

He raised the window.

TRAP

Tommy collected rubber bands from the art closet of his sixth-grade classroom. At home, he looped one rubber band through another, then another, then another, until he'd connected over a dozen rubber bands and made one long, knotted band that he couldn't stretch tight even if he opened his arms out wide. In the backyard, he tested it on the pine tree. Twice around, it fit snugly. He slid his finger between the rubber bands and the bark as if he were testing the waistband on a new pair of suit pants. He pulled, and released, and it snapped back to a good snug fit.

He ran the blade of a box cutter along the bottom of a shoebox and sliced out a narrow rectangle just wide enough for his hand to reach through easily without getting caught up on the edges. He turned the box upright and wriggled his fingers inside its walls. He was reminded of Thing on *The Addams Family*.

He rode his bike to Klosty's Hardware on Broadway in Rocky Point and bought a ball of lightly waxed household string, a narrow gauge that felt like wire between his fingers. He loved the feel of certain things between his fingers: Play-Doh, dry snot, the pads on the paws of his Doberman.

Back home, he rolled a length of string out on the lawn and it performed as he'd hoped, sliding down between blades of grass and under tufts of dandelions and weeds. The little that failed to sink remained inconspicuous—it was the color of faded pine needles, and there were plenty of those lying around on the lawn. His father always told him, "Rake that shit up, you lazy fat bastard." Sometimes he did. Today wasn't one of those times. Tommy had other things on his mind. He pulled sharply on the string, and the slack end responded with sufficient speed—not exactly like the crack end of a bullwhip, he thought, but fast enough for his purposes.

At his father's workbench in the garage, he used a pen file to saw a shallow groove into one end of a six-inch wooden ruler—another item courtesy of the art closet. Kids from the block rolled by on Stingrays and three-speed Schwinns, base-ball cards snapping in the spokes. "Hey Tommy," they called, "you fat fuck." He pulled the garage door closed.

With a hammer and awl, he tapped a small hole into the ruler's other end. He struck a match, lit a candle, and dangled one end of the waxed string in the candle's flame. It singed and curled into a thick ball, like a fist at the end of an arm. He pulled the string's clean end through the hole all the way until the burnt end grabbed. He yanked at it, and the burnt end held firm.

It pleased Tommy to see how efficiently he'd made the hole and the knob at the string's end. With hand tools, fire, and a little ingenuity, he'd created something simple, yet complex. He took care with his work, and that care—the planning and the methodical execution—was in itself satisfying. It wasn't all instant gratification, like his father always accused him of seeking. "You're a slave to your appetites," his father told Tommy every time he looked for snacks in the breadbox or the refrigerator. He called Tommy a lazy slob, a graceless oaf, a water buffalo, and a lummox with two thumbs, a pair of left feet, and a sloppy fat gut. His teachers said much the same, in different words. His shop teacher used the same words.

Now he tested his tools on the back lawn. He stood the ruler on its string end, and inserted an edge of the shoebox into the other end's shallow groove. It settled firmly enough to hold, but not to get stuck. He payed out the free string until he reached a patch of lawn behind privet hedges. He stretched out on his belly, closed one eye as if he were sighting, and visualized the scene, zeroing in like a telescope on the box. He summoned his patience, mastered his breath, and waited for exactly the right moment, then yanked sharply at the string. And it was beautiful—the ruler flying away from the box bottom end first, and the box dropping firmly onto the lawn. Tommy shot from his position like a sprinter off blocks and stuck his hand through the slot of the empty box. He clocked it all in under five seconds.

It was getting dark, and he'd been too much of a presence on the lawn for too long. Things might be watching, wondering. He placed the ruler and the length of rubber bands into his modified box, and set them on a shelf in his closet alongside the Winchester 1029S model pellet rifle he'd received for his birthday.

No one was home.

He filled a glass with cold milk and pulled a Ring Ding from the breadbox.

In the recreation room downstairs, he turned on the television and watched Captain Jack McCarthy introduce *Popeye* cartoons. Then he watched Officer Joe Bolton introduce *The Three Stooges*. Abbot and Costello were next. He got more milk and a package of Yankee Doodles. *Where the Action Is* started at four thirty. He liked the songs of Tommy Roe and Paul Revere and the Raiders, but he couldn't imagine hanging around with the kinds of people who hung around on that show. The guys in white velour turtlenecks, the girls in white go-go boots. Sometimes he watched *Where the Action Is* with his Winchester 1029S in his arms. He drew beads on the slender wholesome dancers and imagined plinking pinch-waisted Gamo Red Fire .177 caliber pellets off their shining white teeth.

At five thirty he clipped a leash on his Doberman. To get to the woods he had to pass by the touch football game at the end of the block. "Hey Tommy, you want to play?" one kid asked him. Another said, "Yeah, we need a fat fuck to be automatic hiker." They all laughed and high-fived until Tommy pretended to unleash the Doberman.

The next day he got home from school and took two slices of Wonder Bread from the breadbox. He tore the slices into small pieces. He got his rifle, his box, his rubber bands, and carried everything out to the yard. He set the rifle behind the privet hedge, the barrel resting in a bipod. He measured off fifteen steps from the hedge, set the box on the lawn, and slipped its edge into the grooved ruler. He payed out the string and dropped the slack behind the hedge. He scattered pieces of Wonder Bread on the lawn while surveying the branches in the nearby scrub oak and scrap pine. The sun hung about two o'clock on the horizon. The box's open end threw a shadow. Inside the box, a patch of sun shone through the slot. He sprinkled bread pieces in the shadow, then up to and under the lid. He placed the choicest morsels in the gleaming patch of sun.

He retreated to his position behind the hedge.

In a few minutes, the birds arrived. Robins, a cardinal, a couple of sparrows, blue jays, starlings. They pecked at the bread. Some beaked up pieces and flew off, others beaked and chewed, then beaked and chewed some more. The big birds chased the little birds, and the little birds chased the crumbs.

The Winchester 1029S came equipped with a 3-9x32 scope. Tommy watched the birds through the sight. He loved the smooth, sleek feel of the thumbhole in the stock, and how that helped the trigger to pull soft as velour. He fingered the trigger and imagined the muffled *thppp* of a pellet piercing a starling's crop, the chaos of wings that would cause, every bird lifting in panic even before the starling's beak bit the dirt. In close-up, the birds looked gluttonous like dogs at a bowl. He looked up over the scope, and almost all the bread he'd thrown was gone. Now the cardinal made its way toward the box's shadow. It nipped, and nipped some more, until there was nothing left but what was under the box, in that patch of golden sun. Without a thought, it seemed, the cardinal slipped under the box.

Tommy caught his breath. He waited a moment, then another, then another, his heart pounding. Then, he yanked and leapt forward.

The box was moving on its own, an inch this way, an inch that. He could hear the cardinal's wings slapping into the cardboard, see its head slam into the narrow slot.

He dropped to his knees and stilled the box with a hand. Peering through the slot, he said, "Hello there, you worthless red fuck."

He stuck his hand through the slot and felt around until he had the bird in his fingers. Its wings strained against his fingers, a soft purposeful feeling. He lifted it, box and all, and with his free hand pulled a loop of rubber bands up over the bird's tail feathers, then higher, over the crinkly witch-like claws of its little feet, and finally around its wings.

He held it up close to his face. The black marble eyes, the

crimson beak. Tremors shook the length of its body, the tiny heart beating wildly in his fingers. It must have been the size of a bb. He felt like he could break the bird's ribcage with a flick of his finger, it was that brittle, that fragile.

A black goatee of feathers surrounded the crimson beak. The beak intrigued him. It had a bit of an overbite. He took it between his fingers and rolled it the way he'd rolled the wire, appreciating the hard matte surface. It reminded him of his father's toenails. He tapped it and the bird shit, and shit again. Some of the shit streaked the sleeves of Tommy's flannel shirt, but he didn't seem to mind.

"That's right," Tommy said, wiping it on his jeans. "Laugh now, cocksucker."

He switched the bird to his free hand, pulled the box from his wrist, and dropped it to the lawn. He carried the bird to the pine tree. He wrapped the length of rubber bands once around the trunk, set the bird in the middle, then looped it around once more. At the bird's waist, he pulled the slack end through one rubber band and doubled-back, like he was cinching a belt. He tested the fit with his finger, its back edge against the cardinal's heaving belly.

He thought about the time he needed a new suit for confirmation. His parents took him to Robert Hall. The salesman wrapped a yellow measuring tape around Tommy's waist and whistled. "Holy smokes, thirty-three inches already?" he said. "Somebody likes his SpaghettiOs, am I right?" Other salesmen laughed. He led them to the racks labeled "Husky." Tommy tried on suit after suit, each more uncomfortable than the last.

"How much can you let out the waist?" his mother asked.

The salesman shrugged, he suggested suspenders. "He keeps the jacket buttoned, no one will see the pants don't zip."

Tommy stepped back from the pine. He studied his prisoner—the brilliant red bird with the crimson beak cinched backside tight against the black sappy bark, the belt of rubber bands digging into its belly feathers.

"You had to go for that last piece of bread," Tommy said, "right? Just a slave to your appetite. So how's it feel now? You good? You full?" He snapped the rubber bands and the bird shit again. "How's that fit, you fat lazy slob of a fuck?" He turned for his rifle.

"Remember," he continued, "you want it snug but comfy. Never buy something you have to break in. Make sure it's comfortable before you leave the store. Only you can tell how it fits. It looks comfortable to me, but I'm not wearing it. Try for a full range of movement. Does it catch anywhere? Restrict? Bunch at the shoulders? A little tight is too tight. You shouldn't even know you're wearing it. Sure, it's a little big now, but the way you're going, you'll grow into it. If I can't see it, no one else can. Trust me."

The 1029S was a break action model. He stuck the butt against his thigh, cocked, loaded, locked. It fired .177 caliber pellets at a velocity of one thousand feet per second. Barely taking aim, he sprayed a few rounds into the bark above the cardinal. Bark chips flew out in all directions, the pellets slammed through the bark and disappeared into the trunk. With this kind of power and velocity, Tommy believed he could take down a cat. Dogs, too, up to maybe a beagle. Even a poodle, one of those medium-size jokes just back from the shop with its ridiculous curls clipped and its taut slender torso shaved clean.

He took his position fifteen steps from the pine tree. He brought the rifle butt up to his shoulder, the barrel cool in his left hand. He closed one eye and zeroed in through the scope.

There it was, a huge red splotch in the crosshairs. It didn't move—it couldn't, but it sure looked like some serious effort was going on under the feathers. The tail, though, that fluttered, and the bark below it was shit-streaked white, gray, green, and black. It looked like one of those pylons at the harbor, which squads of seagulls shit off all day. Tommy drew his bead, and the cardinal shit again. How much shit could there be in one little bird, Tommy wondered. If he kept the bird under his sights much longer, it might shit off half its body weight. It might shit off so much weight, he'd lose two, maybe three inches off his waist. If that happened, he'd fly right out of his trap.

BEFORE AND AFTER SCIENCE

I stumble in half-pissed and Shelley's on the phone. Of my three female roommates, Shelley is the least attractive. She's got lovely tits and a decent collection of classical records with an emphasis on early music, but she's well-adjusted, a condition that makes my sort nervous, and on her throat, just above the collarbone is this leech-like lump the length of a penny roll that she conceals only somewhat successfully under high collars and turtlenecks. It's Indian summer now, and her neckline is low. There's a good two, two-and-a-half inches of cleavage showing, but then there's that awful leechy blotch dangling like the spider above Little Miss Muffett's curds and whey. The old pull and push. I'm attracted and repulsed, and a bit disgusted at being repulsed. It's impractical for one: these are beautiful and readily available tits. And then of course two: judging someone's personal worth on the basis of what amounts to the merest percentage of total skin area is shallow, to say the least, but there it is; I'm like a dog with a hunk of fat off the barbecue—I know it's good, and I know I want it, I want it now, but it burns my tongue so badly all I can do is yelp, not chew, and that makes me angry.

So Shelley's on the phone and I'm half-pissed. Actually, I'm very-near-thoroughly-pissed. And I'm attracted, repulsed, disgusted, and angry. I have this thing about women on the phone. Like Niagara Falls to me—"slowly I turn . . ." It goes back to my mother, who I see before me now with a phone receiver staple-gunned to her cheek, pressing the buttons of a wall model touchtone with a pencil's pink nub. In this picture, I'm looking up imploringly with both hands cupped at the crotch of my tan corduroys. A question—and it's a good one—arises: Why then do I choose to people my apartment with college and grad-school aged women who—one might assume and correctly I might add—spend an inordinate amount of time on the telephone yakking. For now, in this very-near-thoroughly-pissed state, I can only aver this: I'm re-evaluating.

"It's okay, Jenn," Shelley is saying. "Try to get some sleep." She rolls her eyes at me. "Jenn, it gets better, Jenn, I promise."

"Is that Jenn?" I say, as if my question results from some penetrating detection. I've heard these calls before. Shelley is like a suicide hotline. All her Barnard friends are ready to jump out windows, an option not readily available to Shelley. We live on the ground floor. Maybe that's why they call her. But I'm not concerned with the motivations of chronically depressed Barnard upperclasswomen. Instead, I'm thinking about Film Production II, and Jenn's appearance in a col-league's 16mm short, the obligatory nude-romp-in-the-cemetery sequence, and I grab at the phone.

"Jenn, hold on," Shelley says as I paw the receiver.

"Jenn, are you home," I say impatiently. I've got the phone in one hand, I'm straight-arming Shelley with the other, the palm flat out on her shoulder, a misplacement which renders the straight-arm ineffectual. See, even though I want to keep Shelley off me, I've got the presence of mind to avoid that blotch. I'm squeamish, a quality I find nauseating and unmanly. It prevents me from getting what I think I want.

"Don't tell him, Jenn," Shelley shouts into the receiver.

I give Shelley a look, but it's not necessary. Jenn's not paying attention.

"And Shelley has your address?" I say.

I nod and hang up before she stops talking. Never give them time to think. The mind is a monkey, especially when it's enrolled in an all-girls college.

"I don't know about this," Shelley says, shaking her head.

"Shell," I tell her, "she's lonely. So am I."

Shelley's got her arms folded, but not high enough to conceal that splotch. "There's another word for what you are," she says.

"Don't flatter me now, Shelley, please." I slide a pink highlighter and a yellow 3x5 card along the kitchen table. "Chivalry," I say, "can't wait. The Arthurians knew this."

Shelley's period is medieval. She doesn't know whether to smile or puke. Still shaking her head, she takes up the highlighter.

"One of us is going to regret this," she says.

She leans an elbow against the kitchen table, affording me a full view of her ample chest. In my head I hear the love-cry of Hitchcock's *Frenzy*, the teeth-clenched urgency of the murderer's kiss-off: "Lovely," he moans. "Lovely!"

On Riverside Drive I take the shadowy promenade above the park. There's a professor I'm trying to date two doors down and I don't want her to see me rushing off on some half-baked tryst carrying a half-drunk double-litre of Folonari. Folonari's piss, a judgment I'm sure she shares. She's got class, this professor, a Katherine Hepburn type. Trouble is, she's suicidal, too. Wrote a book on it, it's her claim to fame. More attempts than Sylvia Plath, one less success. Next failure they'll make her the dean, you can take that to the bank. One night right outside my window, there she is braless and carrying on, howling at the street sign about some injustice, until finally she melts into this little puddle like the Wicked Witch of the West after Dorothy's doused her with water. I forgo the chemise and leap out the window and against her protests escort her back to her building, where against my protests some little prick of a doorman takes over. Grandly, he covers her torso with the blazer of his monkey suit. A regular Ivanhoe. Still, tucked into the elevator, I knew where his eyes were going to be traveling. That's a funny thing about men: bad tits, good tits, vital or suicidal, we're gonna look. I've looked down the blouses of grandmothers leaning over strollers. I've lifted my eyes from the *Times* to the monkey bars. I can't say I'm not disgusted with myself, but I'm not not looking.

It's one of those damp clammy nights. I've got a blazer around my shoulders, my tie ends dangle from a half-assed Windsor. Casual but ready, you might say. My upstairs neighbors, another professor and his wife, both painters, pass by with their leashed whippets. Although the whippets strain at their collars to greet me, my neighbors pretend not to notice. I used to date their daughter who, once she got the full impact of my number, told them I was running some kind of harem downstairs. "Pussy pig," she called me, and I didn't bother to argue. We split up nasty and they sent her off to Barcelona, whence I began receiving post cards imploring my visit. She's learned so much about appearance, she says, both scientific and natural, she's certain we can work out our differences. And this really gets me. I mean, there she is, across an ocean, halfway around a planet, I couldn't see her with a telescope, and she's still concerned about whether or not my critical ass finds her appealing. Weird, I think, and sad. Of course, that insecurity's got its upside, but the reference to science worries me.

Women struggle these days, and I feel bad about my ugly contribution to their burden. I see them crunching, fasting, applicating crèmes. Eleven p.m. and there they go, look out there's a whole flock of them. Jesus what they go through. Late night joggers earning centiliters of frozen yogurt, watching for wackos, shying from Rottweilers, edging around pigeons preening at puddles. Once I leapt the width of a not-so-large promenade puddle and killed a pigeon, or at least I think I killed it. Came down right on its breastbone. Sickening crackle. Half-shocked me. I couldn't imagine the stupid bird not scatting. I suppose it, too, was suicidal. In that case, I did it a favor. Imagine finally working up the nerve to jump from the window only to discover wings flapping at your sides.

I had a chance, once, to be some kind of crusader. My brother had come home from college with a dog-eared copy of *Sisterhood is Powerful*. I remember thinking, wow, some of this shit is right on! But I got tired of dating women in hooded sweatshirts and earth clogs. My erections required greater glamour. More and more my eyes lingered on the magazine displays at kiosks (among which Shelley could hold her own were it not for that unfortunate marking). So call me counter-progressive, call me a throwback, and I say: What, you think I'm proud of this? I'm not proud of this, it's just something I do. I agree with you. It's myself I'm in disagreement with, but I'm still myself.

Jenn lives on 108th St. I take the Riverside service lane at 110th, nose around the corner, hugging the shadows. A scaffold doglegs 109th and RSD. Local Law 10. Evidently there's more falling from windows than Barnard students. Bricks, flowerboxes, gargoyles. Scaffolds going up everywhere, New York City masquerading as a French museum, the buildings wearing infrastructure on the outside, like Madonna's costumes.

In winter, when the wind gets fierce and glass sheets rip right out of frames, the scaffolds offer refuge. Now, though, in these clammy days of September, the scaffolds seem more of a mugger's haven.

Which is appropriate, I suppose, since I'm feeling like a criminal. I hardly know Jenn, I've met her only twice. The first time I thoroughly ignored her. She was sitting in my kitchen doing tea readings with Shelley, looking like any number of nondescript Barnard girls. Straight hair, calf-length skirt, lace-up ankle-high Wicca boots. A self-conscious refusal to smile, presentation of self vacillating between Patti Smith and Barbara Seagull. But later I caught her in that student film. She played Salome in a pixilated adaptation of the *Dance of the Seven Veils*, only Jenn hadn't used any, veils that is, except her waist-length hair at times acted as one. But at other times it didn't, and Jenn had mouthwatering breasts, or so they appeared in the low-budget, spurt-shot, strobe-lit effects, and she knew how to toss them all over the screen. Next time I see her, at Cannon's bar, I buy her a beer and we talk. French lit, French film. I try for a date, *Pierrot le fou* at the Thalia, but she works nights at St. Luke's. I joke about access to drugs, she's serious. "Whatever I can get my hands on," she says, air-thumbing a hypo into her elbow's pit, her eyes going loopy.

On Jenn's stoop a couple of homeboys pose tough in front of the columns of buzzers. I'm reminded of Shelley's last plea.

"Are you sure about this?" she'd asked, handing me Jenn's address on the 3x5 card.

I said, "About what?"

"Don't give me that," Shelley said, "she's really nuts."

"Who isn't?" I said.

"You know what I mean," Shelley said. "And you're not

nuts, you're despicable. There's a difference. This girl's fragile, she's made three attempts." Then she said, "Stay with me. I can just call her back."

And that of course was the wrong thing to say, because if she agreed now she'd agree another time, she was money in the bank. Jenn was another matter.

When I pulled out the Folonari, Shelley said, "Topher, this isn't you."

"I know it, love," I told her, winking and tapping at my wrist-watch, "but the liquor stores are closed."

She answers the door in a set of over-large coveralls, the one strap buckled look. Below that, a sleeveless t-shirt, circa Harvey Keitel. It's tight, holey, revealing, overwashed. Her breasts appear solid as a pair of binoculars. In one hand, she carries a pair of seamstress's shears, from the other dangles what appears to be a scalp. Perhaps only minutes, seconds earlier, her long straight hair had hung to her waist. Now, blunt prominent bangs retreat from her eyebrows. She looks like Suzanne Vega in Oregon. I hate Suzanne Vega, mixed feelings about Oregon. But the breast thing, of course, that intrigues.

"You coming in?" she asks, turning into the apartment.

"Wait a second," I say, grabbing her arm. She looks at me dispassionately. "You like Suzanne Vega?" I say.

She says, "Suzanne who?"

"Good," I say, "carry on."

She leads me down a brown corridor lined with bookshelves ready to crumple under their burdens of books and dust.

"I'm doing something in the bathroom," she tells me. "Make yourself at home."

The apartment is cavernous, rooms leading off rooms

leading off hallways. The color scheme is the browns and grays of cubism. The mood is Munch. Above an antique employed as a telephone stand, a black and white Molly Ringwald poster is tacked off-angle.

"Are we alone?" I ask.

"My roommates are gone," she says, "for the weekend."

I ask her does she want some wine.

"Whatever," she tells me.

I take my time finding the kitchen. The books run the typical gamut. There's the Janson's, the Djuna Barnes, the New Directions H.D., *Our Bodies Our Selves*. I'd given that tome more than the once over. A veritable gallery of pussy pictures. Each one different, its own person like, yet each as disembodied as the most objectified Larry Flynt. Of course, the publishers' intentions differ. I realize that I experience my life like some of my favorite music, a Mendelssohn *Romance sans paroles*. An argument advanced, then its antithesis, then . . . another argument, a theme and variation, synthesis never achieved. Sometimes I wonder if I'm still trying.

The dust in this corridor is like silt in a shipwreck. I kick up tiny clouds every step, my nose feels clogged. Despite that, I detect the presence of cats, a number of them.

In the kitchen I hit a light switch. Roaches scurry and I swear furballs fly. Near the refrigerator a roach, or a waterbug if you want to get technical, props itself on its forelegs, its head bent into a saucer of water. I actually hear it drinking, it is that big. It turns its head to look at me, a once-over like, then resumes its drinking, as if it's said, "Oh, it's you." Below a windowsill a cat litter box overflows with turds. The floor, scattered with Friskies and Kitty Kleen, is like walking on Rice Krispies.

There is nothing, absolutely nothing in the icebox except

cat food and cans of Tab. In the cabinets I find more Tab and bags of pretzels, dozens of them. Veri-thins. I hear something up above the cupboard and my heart starts. A large Tomcat stretches, then jumps down.

"Meow," he says, and makes a headpost of my legs.

I noticed he's castrated. Disgusted, I say, "Yeah?" and flick him a pussful of Folonari. He scats to a corner, alternately shaking and licking his whiskers.

Music comes faintly from so far away it sounds like the soundtrack to a movie in another apartment's VCR. A tortured soundtrack, all gnarled and angular. "The Transfigured Night," perhaps, or the "Grosse Fuge." It's so faint that it's hard to get a fix, but I get the picture. Olive trees in winter, naked yearning branches reaching into a low sunless sky. I wonder if it's been on all along, or if Jenn just put it on. Is it a reflection of her condition, or of her hopes for the evening? A little artist-formerly-known-as-Prince would have been a more positive, if less subtle, sign. I go in the opposite direction, down a hall, another hall, a bathroom.

More roaches, another cat litter box, more Rice Krispies linoleum. I'm tempted to piss in the sink but I refrain, although I don't know what stops me. There's a barely contained hostility in all of this catting around, and one must learn its symbolic language. The appropriate gesture, the well-tempered sneer, the right dose of humiliation, these create the frisson, the hilarity, the giddy danger.

The medicine chest's second shelf is lined with a row of unboxed diaphragms, a warehouse of flying saucers. I feel as though I'm looking at a Magritte. Expectation collides with actuality. This is commonly thought to produce revelations. All I get is anxious.

The diaphragms are of various sizes but all, against the pictorial evidence of *Our Bodies, Our Selves*, relatively the same. Do they share them? Interchange them? Are they for different times in the month? I remove a couple, holding them by the tips of my fingers. They're vanilla caked in a kind of map-like relief, a silt of corn starch and ortho-crème aged to the color of cardboard. The convex sides smell like nitrous oxide, the concave chlorine. I slide them back in in no particular order. I feel one of those alcoholic headaches coming on comprised as much of bad choices regrettably yet to be made as of the alcohol. The kind of headache where the hangover precedes the debauch and the head, the actual brain case, seems to swell. I make sure the Tylenol jar contains Tylenol and I wash down three extra-strength tablets with the Folonari.

In a dark bedroom I find a phone and dial my own number. I want something from Shelley, but I'm not certain what it is. To save Jenn from me? To save me from me? I don't think for a second that because I've read Proust and can locate the three-act structure in *Claire's Knee*, I'm any different from the slobs in a volunteer firehouse hog-hosing strippers on the pool table and then popping another keg. But I want to be. I do want to be. But the line's busy.

I'm sitting on pillows at the head of the bed. The headboard is one of those brass antique jobs, the narrow coiled bars like a jail cell's rising into the shape of a harp. Along the mattress I check for handcuff scuffs; this looks like a heavy hitter's dream. It's separated from the windowsill by a plank-covered floor radiator stacked with books. I call for the time and the weather, then I call information for Jenn's number. Jenn Korngold, I tell the operator. As I suspected, it's a different number from the phone I'm on. When roommates don't like each other, they get separate numbers. I can't imagine anyone getting along well with Jenn.

In the distance, a phone rings four, five times. The ringing is replaced by silence.

"Jenn," I say into the receiver, "I'm lost, Jenn. Follow the sound of my voice. Find me, Jenn."

Jenn is barefoot but I hear the sandpapery shuffle of her feet over the scritchy-scratchy floors. Lights flash on and off, faint lights as if ice boxes open and close.

"I can't hear you," Jenn says. "Say something."

"Something."

"Something intelligent."

"Take off your blouse."

"In another language."

"*Deshabiller, s'il vous plait.*"

When she appears, she's topless. She's also practically bald. I flick on a nightstand light and she makes no move to cover herself. Her hands are full. From one finger dangles a seltzer dispenser, the other hand supports a box of Whipmaster N^2O cartridges.

"This is Carla's room," she says. She takes a lotus position at the foot of the bed. She lifts the canister to her lips and presses a long whoosh of N^2O into her lungs. Her eyes scrunch, her shoulders relax. I notice for the first time that she wears a nose ring. Also a nipple ring. Around each ring is a little bead of blood. Her breasts are unimaginably perfect.

"You wanted me to take off my blouse," she says through a smile. Her eyes remain closed, inviting me to drink in her image as impersonally as if she were a spread in a magazine. "You must have seen my movie."

"They're perfect," I say, a bad move, but I can't disguise the awe. "More perfect than I imagined."

She chuckles. "They ought to be," she says. "They cost enough."

"You mean—"

She nods, then takes another pull from the canister.

"Do you mind?" I ask her.

She shakes her head and smiles.

While I knead and suck and mutter exclamations, she goes through another half-dozen cartridges. At one point, she gets up and presses a cassette into a boombox. She doesn't ask what I'd like to hear. She doesn't ask if I'd like to hear anything. It's Brian Eno, *Before and After Science*, the dreamy multi-tracked side that opens with "Here He Comes." It sounds the way anesthesia feels. She resumes with the gas, inhaling deeply, rocking gently. She doesn't offer me a pull. She doesn't offer the slightest response to my attentions. It's as if I'm not even there. I lift her tits, pinch them, pull them, press them together, spread them apart. I nip the circumference of what appears to be a tender area around the ring. Even that fails to produce a wince. Their firmth, if you like, is what one hopes for, dreams of, desires, but rarely if ever encounters except with teenagers and often not even with them. I can see the thin razor lines below the nipples where the silicon's been inserted. I trace the lines with my lips, my fingertips. I'm fascinated and repulsed. The changing expressions on her face have everything to do with the laughing gas, nothing at all to do with my slobbering. And her profound distraction has an extraordinary effect on me. I don't know if I've ever felt this excited.

I coax her out of her coveralls, but it's less a seduction than a desire not to wake a somnambulist. This is getting into weird territory ethically, but it's new and I can't stop. She's not suicidal, she's crazy, and infinitely desirable. And she does exhibit evidence of will and consciousness. When I try to remove her panties she says no. When I discover the same razor thin lines on her thighs and her sides, she explains, briefly, that she'd been a fat teenager who finally convinced her parents to pay for cosmetic surgery.

I introduce the idea of a "pearl necklace," and the idea intrigues her long enough to get her to lie down and press her surgically enhanced tits around my cock. Her head's on the pillows, too high up, but rather than disturb her I squeeze my own head through the bars of the headboard. Grasping the headposts, I keep steady and my eyes stare directly down onto a paperback copy of Chinua Achebe's *Things Fall Apart*. Luckily, all this weirdness has me so jazzed up I climax in a minimum of strokes. An agonizing splurt, a gusher, a thorough voiding of the lower chakra, all over her clavicle, her neck, and chin. Through it she giggles like a child, guileless, delighted, surprised. The second my squirming stops she's over at the mirror above Carla's dresser.

"Do you always come this much?" she asks.

I try to turn my head, but it only goes so far.

"Wait," I tell her, "I can't see." I try to pull back, but the pressure on my head's too great. "I think I'm stuck."

I pull straight back, back at an angle. I try the upper part of the headboard slot, then I try the lower. I can only move my head up and down, not back and out. When I pull back, it feels as if my ears might rip right off my head.

Jenn resumes her position on the edge of the bed. Or, should I say, she resumes her manner, I can't see if she's in the same position. I feel her weight on the bed, I hear the whooshes of the gas, the drones of *Before and After Science*. But all I see is thin slat Venetian blinds and the Chinua Achebe novel.

Between cartridges she says, "Your hiney hole looks funny."

"Very funny," I tell her.

"No," she says, "not very funny. Funny. You have a hemorrhoid, do you know that?"

I feel my face flush.

She touches the hemorrhoid with what feels like a finger. The feeling is humiliating and pleasurable at once. I ask her if Carla has ever come home early.

"Sometimes," she says. "She's unpredictable."

I ask her to bring me a couple of Tylenols. She returns with the bottle and what looks like a makeup kit.

"What are you doing?" I ask her.

She's snickering, and I feel a tickling around my ass.

In a high squeaky voice, she says, "Hello, Mr. Hiney Hole. Does Mr. Hiney Hole like gerbils?" She sounds like one of those faces people paint between the thumb and forefinger. She laughs so hard I imagine her clutching her stomach.

"Wait," I say, "what are you doing?"

"Shh," she says. "I'm talking to Mr. Hiney Hole. I think he's got a temperature." She resumes the high voice. "Mr. Hiney Hole, you look a little piqued. Do you have a temperature?"

Her finger or something like one jams halfway up my ass, and my shoulders crash into the headboard like I'm hitting a tackling dummy.

"Jenn, what the fuck are you doing?"

"Shhh," she calms me, but I yank back so hard that my ears rip where the lobes meet the neckline. First there's a dry stinging, then a trickle of blood. The blood tickles my jawline.

"See?" she says, "you're bleeding. Now shhh."

"Get me out of this goddamn thing," I say. "Jenny, now!" I try to Samson the headboard's rods out from my neck but succeed only in whitening my knuckles and reddening my face. I don't know if it's sweat or blood trickling across the back of my fist.

"You're getting yourself all excited," Jenn says, "and the more you squirm the more medicine Mr. Hiney Hole requires."

"Whatever you're thinking of doing, Jenn, you better stop."

I feel something cool and wet on a cotton puff. "Shh shh shh shh shh shh shh," she says.

"Jenn?"

A sharp needle prick follows, then a warmth, a liquid warmth. A heat. The heat sparkles white, then blue, red, red-orange. I remember my fists falling open . . .

I wake up in piercing sunlight film-noired by the blinds. My mouth is dry as dead skin, the head around it the size of a medicine ball and about as heavy. The Chinua Achebe novel is covered in drool. Alongside that is a note weighted by an adjustable wrench and a set of keys.

"Thanks," the note reads. "I needed that. You were a scream. I haven't laughed so hard since French Lit II with Lotringer." Instructions for leaving the apartment follow. Where could she be, I wonder? Temple? A PS appears at the bottom. "Please feed Mr. Richard his breakfast. His can's on the counter." She signed with a small smile in a huge head. Very funny.

The wrench works, but it's a struggle. The hexagonal nuts at the bottom of each rod are small. I can't see what I'm doing, my neck hurts, and I manage only quarter turns before my knuckles slam into the adjacent rods. Plus, my head pounds and I'm sweating like a woman in delivery. Ten, fifteen minutes I'm loose. Mr. Richard sleeps at my side, or had. My movements disturb him. He meows, then purrs. Evidently

I'm forgiven. Either that or he loves Folonari. Suddenly I'm suspicious of the cat: Was he in on this act, whatever it was? I recall a scene in an early John Waters' film in which a woman's boyfriend fucks her with the head of a live chicken. I rub Mr. Richard's head and it's reassuringly free of lubricant. So are his paws.

I fist Tylenol into my mouth, guzzle water from the bathroom faucet, vomit. I have never felt sicker in my life. The Folonari's at least partially to blame, but just partially. I try to match the symptoms with something else I've experienced, something I know about other drugs. But I can't. I'm wobbly as a hog on ice, and my eyes are glassy and bloodshot, the pupils as distant as a pair of pennies at the bottom of a pool. There's a smell inside my nose, I'm not picking it up, I'm it. It's chemical, clinical, medicinal, sour. I puke again. The usual mantras follow, all beginning with "never again." In the agony of the moment I'd almost swear I mean them.

In the medicine chest mirror I try to see my ass but I can't turn my head. A field goal specialist couldn't kick my neck loose. I feel the hole, Mr. Hiney Hole. It is moist and sore, but there's nothing in it—anymore. Mr. Richard rubs at my ankles.

I get dressed quickly but carefully, skip the tie, give Mr. Richard's head a scratch. There's a detail I'll foreground in my version for Shelley.

In the kitchen I crack open a can of "Liverbits & Tuna" and almost sick up in the sink. Outside the apartment I have a choice, but I'm re-evaluating. I follow Jenn's instructions. First the upper lock, then the lower. Mr. Hiney Hole indeed. I slide both keys under the apartment door. This, I feel, even while performing it, is the greatest humiliation.

PARIS

She was rear-ended coming off Carrolton Avenue at the corner of Dumaine. The collision was not high speed, but the damage was significant: the trunk folded like an accordion, and the rear windshield cracked in a jagged puzzle. The rear axle, however, remained intact, as did the differential. A mechanic assured her that the car remained drivable without repair.

Her insurance company offered her twenty-six-hundred dollars in damages. But the damage, her boyfriend insisted, was cosmetic. He was an older guy from up north with tattoos in foreign alphabets and a pair of advanced university degrees in disciplines that turned out to pay dick. "Damage is character," he told her, "and character is formed by experience, not smooth fenders. So fuck repairs. Let's go to Paris." She took the insurance money and purchased round trip tickets on Air France.

Paris was a dream for her—she was twenty-one, from Kentucky. The only body of water she'd ever crossed was the Ohio River. She'd never been farther east than Cleveland. Once, in Community College, a professor had assigned *The Flowers of Evil*. From that text, she formed an impression of Paris as a vast garden of opiated deceit and decadent enslavement to passion. Now, she would tour the book's landscape, with a guide who'd actually read it in its original language. Her boyfriend once lived in Paris. He knew how to stretch limited resources into unlimited weeks of travel and habitation in foreign cities.

Her roommate drove them to the airport in the rear-ended car.

"Be careful," the roommate told her.

The boyfriend said, "That's what I'm here for." He patted the pockets of his vest—four of them, stuffed with boarding passes, passports, and cash. Her new camera dangled from a strap over his shoulder.

She got airsick on the flight. The boyfriend moved to an empty seat near the cabin's front. When they deplaned, he wasn't waiting at the end of the loading bridge. She didn't see him on the long walk from the exit to immigration. He had been carrying everything except the books she'd brought along to read. He'd once told her that he experienced periods of constipation followed by diarrhea. Maybe he'd eaten something on the flight, then rushed to a restroom where he might still be passing waste. She sat against a wall and took out her *Lonely Planet*. She'd marked the page with Baudelaire's tomb.

Half an hour later a customs official prodded her shoulder. Communication was a struggle, but she gathered, finally, that she should produce a passport. How could she explain that her boyfriend with the irregular bowels kept all her documents?

The customs official led her to a brightly lit waiting room where several women in headscarves muttered in a strange language. One of the women had been crying. She wanted to assure the crying woman that everything would work out for the best, that experience formed character.

BLASPHEMY

My girlfriend wakes and joins me in the kitchen, where I sit contemplating my dreams. I've been having a series of disturbing ones, most of them having to do with me and my girlfriend. I haven't told her any. Last night's dream is different, but equally troubling.

She lights the flame below the kettle for coffee. I ask her if she wants to help decode my dream. Without responding, she points to the bathroom and leaves.

I put on some music by Ravel, the dreamy solo piano works, and open a collection of stories by Peter Cameron, but my dream, and my girlfriend's dismissal of it, niggle.

The dream concerns a fishing trip. I don't fish. It's with my girlfriend. She won't even eat fish. There are some Mormons present (do Mormons fish? I wonder), and they accuse me of blasphemy. I've done, or haven't done, something with the fish.

At Barney's, I ask a lawyer about this. We are crouched in an aisle amidst racks of empty suits. The lawyer looks at the fish—there are three of them, silvery with a green tint, hooks still in their mouths—and listens to my version of events.

My girlfriend approaches, modeling a dark olive overcoat faintly checked in charcoal. The lawyer nods approvingly. I'm ready to offer my approval, too, but I'm waiting for my girlfriend to acknowledge me. She doesn't. Indifferent as a runway model, she spins off down the aisle, her red hair turning a sickly pale blond like Courtney Love's.

"Is she shopping at Barney's?" I ask the lawyer.

The lawyer ignores my question.

"Mormons," he explains, getting back to the fish, "have rituals you failed to follow."

But why the blasphemy charge, I ask him.

He says I'll have a chance to explain if I testify.

"God gave you a choice," he says.

That's just it, I want to say, I don't want to testify, but the lawyer is already gone.

My girlfriend returns from the bathroom. Before I can tell her the dream, the kettle whistles. She fills the French press and carries it, with her journal, to the table.

"I've had so many dreams," she says, already writing. "Filled with strangers. I don't know who these people are."

I wonder if she, too, has dreamed of Mormons. I don't bother to ask.

In the Peter Cameron story I'm reading, a teenage boy refuses to speak. At one point the boy dives into a murky pool looking for a diamond that's come loose from his mother's ring. Later he shares a cherry ice pop with his stepfather, who isn't much older than the boy. The stepfather wears a Disney World t-shirt. Throughout, the boy remains mute.

Ten, fifteen minutes later my girlfriend closes her journal and picks up the phone. One by one she writes down her messages, hangs up, dials a number. One continuous action.

"My brother left a message," she tells me over the receiver. "He said, 'Why aren't you at home sitting by the phone worrying?'"

Her brother, the baby of the family, has had a recent suicidal episode. After six years' sobriety, he'd fallen off the wagon and made cryptic calls to old lovers, who contacted his parents, who contacted my girlfriend. Pistols and ledges were mentioned. My girlfriend was shocked. Apparently there hadn't been any indications of her brother's despair, or else she had failed to hear them. Now they have an agreement. If they haven't spoken during the day, he checks in with her at night so she won't worry.

She gets him at work, and instantly they are laughing. Or at least she is. The phone brings out her mirth.

I finish the Peter Cameron story. The teenage boy's mother complains about his silence, but when he opens his mouth to explain, she covers it with her hand. Her hand smells of chlorine from the pool.

At the sink, I run hot water into the few utensils from last night's dinner, and into the mugs and coffee presses and little plates we've used for this morning's breakfast. I'm wondering about my dream: Who is the lawyer? How come Barney's? Why blasphemy?

Next door, workers arrive. They're renovating the apartment where an elderly woman recently died. Their chatter is loud. Usually the chatter is Spanish. Today it's German. For some reason, I suppose that means plumbers.

The German resounds in the empty apartment and reverberates through my walls. With the water running, and the Germans chattering, and my girlfriend giggling with her suicidal brother on the phone, I can no longer hear the dreamy Ravel.

She hangs up, stands, stretches.

"He sounds a lot better," she tells me.

"Than what?" I say.

Next thing she's fully dressed, her bag hanging from her shoulder.

She says, "I can see you're impatient for me to go."

SHADOW

At the edge of Alice Town, the Shark Lab kept live specimens in wide expansive cages separated by boardwalks that extended into the harbor. At the cage farthest from shore was the largest shark, a lemon tiger nine feet long. The boys watched her patrol the perimeter of the cage, a gray shadow in black water pierced by shafts of light from the nearby clubs and from the floods on pylons. The boys had missed the last water taxi, and their boat, the Evergreen, lay at anchor about two hundred meters from the shark cage. The generator was silent, the lights down, the captain and crew asleep for several hours.

The shark was ceaseless and repetitive and tireless. The boys were drunk and frightened and amused. They had seen sharks before, but each previous sighting had been on the sharks' terms—in the water. The boys had carried Hawaiian slings, and sometimes their mesh catch-bags contained fresh-speared fish. Each time, they'd had to get out of the water quickly, but carefully, and always without their catch. Now, for the first time, they had a shark on their terms, and they taunted her. They threw coins into her cage. When a coin plipped into the water, she zigged in its direction. They'd throw another, and she zagged. The great gray shadow of her looked like a puppet yanked by a drunken master.

Earlier, the boys had visited the Yama Bahama, a brothel one unpaved block inland from Front Street. Charlie selected Aletra, a large dark woman in white underwear. Jeff took Jean, a cinnamon-freckled girl with a narrow waist and full round breasts. In their room, Jeff lay down beneath her but found he was unable to function. "You drink too much Bacardi, mon," she said, feathering his thigh with her soft fingers. But that wasn't it.

He'd remembered something that his father always asked him, a question that seemed to materialize at the most inopportune times. "If you were a character in a movie," his father would ask him, "would the audience love you and really hope that you got what you wanted, or would they think you were just another self-serving puke trying to be cool?"

Since leaving home, Jeff was discovering that there were things inside him he didn't even know what they were, except that in moments of decision they took control. He didn't like it; it was definitely not cool.

Charlie didn't appear to hear such questions. No matter what the situation, he seemed easily able to remain cool. He was physically strong, graceful, sinewy, confident. Intellectually, he was average, or just enough above average to be dissatisfied with his intellect, but unable to do much about it. He was poorly read, and baffled by the literary challenges Jeff tackled. He'd failed out of his first year at BU, despite the high grades he'd received for the papers that Jeff, a high school dropout, wrote for him. Jeff was intellectually strong, widely read, and verbally gifted, but he was physically clumsy, soft and thick around the waist, and embarrassed to be seen without his shirt on. Once, near Great Isaac's Light, Jeff had fled from the water at the sight of a large fish that turned out to have been a bluefin tuna. This had been an event of great amusement to Charlie.

Sounds of music drifted from the Alice Town clubs. James Brown, Chaka Kahn, the Average White Band. The music was fine, but it wasn't what Jeff had hoped to hear—he wanted to hear native music, whatever that was. It disturbed him to see the way the Bahamians on Bimini costumed themselves, the boys in platform shoes and shirts with wide, flashy collars, the girls in brightly colored sateen hot pants and newsboy caps with puffy crowns. These were the styles Jeff had left America to avoid, the styles invented by an industry, not evolved by a culture. He'd thought that if he left America, he'd leave America behind. Instead, he found it everywhere, reflected back at garish angles. When he shared this awareness with his friend, Charlie shrugged. "Dig it," he'd said. "It's the price we pay for being number one."

The boys grew bored of throwing pennies for the shark, not long after the shark had grown bored chasing them. At the last several, she completely ignored the surface disturbances and maintained her dispassionate patrol of the cage's perimeter. Jeff wondered if she was playing possum.

The mosquitoes weren't playing possum, they were finding Jeff's flesh, three, four, five at a time. Charlie seemed unperturbed.

"I can't stay out here all night," Jeff said.

"Then don't," Charlie said. "The boat's a short swim away. Unless you're scared there's some tuna out there."

Jeff looked at his friend. "You know what, man? Fuck you."

Charlie said, "Right back at you, good buddy."

Jeff looked out into the harbor, the Evergreen at anchor, the great dark silhouette of it between its stern and bow lights.

He stepped out of his shorts and yanked the t-shirt over his head. He folded them carefully into a neat square and placed them on his deck shoes. He'd become accustomed to making everything neat and compact. On a boat, that could be the difference between life and death, and Jeff had begun to appreciate the dramatic provenance of habits as mundane as folding one's clothes. He stepped onto the ladder face out and leaned over the water. At that moment, a shadow just like the one in the shark cage, only larger, angled out from below the pier.

"Holy shit," Jeff said, his heart thumping.

"Yeah," Charlie laughed. "He's a big motherfucker, too." He took a last pull off his cigarette and snapped the butt into the shark cage. "So what's it gonna be, hero? Him or the mosquitoes?"

Jeff entered the water one rung at a time, and pushed off the ladder gently. The caged female followed along the edge of her fencing, one slit eye coldly staring.

He closed his eyes and free-styled for several dozen strokes.

He stopped to tread water—he'd gone considerably off course.

When he located the boat, the shadow passed directly beneath him.

He free-styled again. He became immersed in the shadow. He rode it, and it carried him as if he were on a surfboard.

GRÆY AREA

Walking down Broadway, a cool breeze blowing in from the Hudson. A few floors up in one of the student dorms, a flapping white sheet makes that snapping sound you get when the corner of a wet towel snaps against someone's ass. A stenciled slogan fills the sheet. I shield my eyes from the sun and read, "RAPE IS RAPE. THERE IS NO GREY AREA."

Hmm, I think. Grey area—grey with an *E*, not an *A*. Is there any difference in meaning, and if so, what did the sloganeer mean by the *E* and not the *A*, which I think is the spelling of gray I would have chosen—the image of the letter *A* causes the reader to make the "ay" sound. Whereas *E* requires a little mental gymnastics—the reader must translate the "ee" into "ay" sound, unless the reader's French and you're talking about something like "outré," but then you'd need an *accent aigu*, wouldn't you?

I continue down Broadway, past the library and the luncheonette, that Hudson breeze causing a lovely havoc with hemlines. I'm thinking about how stimulating it is to teach up here. The youth, the ideas. I'm thinking about *A*s and *E*s and gray areas and rape. Of course, no one would disagree with that slogan: there is no grey area. But do they agree publicly because they feel compelled to? Because to disagree would cause a huge conflagration? Accusations of sexism? Chauvinism? Misogyny? Only a fool would disagree in public. But my head, I think, is still private, and I start mulling it over. Start raising questions. Is there really no grey area? I remember my anger at the Mike Tyson conviction, the whole Mike Tyson trial. I've been trained to understand that there's a gray area in everything. Everyone is a hero in her own story. Or a victim. Everyone has his own version. *Tout le monde a leurs raisons.*

I had a student, a Barnard girl, I don't know, nineteen, twenty years old. I know—I should call her a woman. Maybe calling her a girl is a form of rape, of perpetuating infantilizing terminology. I don't know—maybe there's a gray area, to everyone but the Andrea Dworkin types. But this girl, this woman, this Barnard junior, she sure seemed like a girl to me. To help pay her way through school, she took a job with some gewgaw boutique on the Upper East Side. An expensive little joint half a block from a post office. The postman who delivered the boutique's mail was Hispanic. Nice guy. Hector. He liked to wear those mailman shorts until it was numbingly cold out. He had thick, muscular calves covered in forests of black hair. Always friendly, quick with a joke, quick with a compliment. This girl—I'll call her Helen—she liked him. As in got a kick out of him. As in enjoyed the feeling she got by being friends with someone from a different culture (Helen was from Minnesota, her mother was an MD, her father a professor), enjoyed the little frisson that came with bantering in Spanish with a Spanish speaker, saying shit right, or at least understandable, getting the jokes, hearing the accent. Hector was no Catalan, that's for sure. Puerto Rican, Dominican, maybe Venezuelan or Columbian. She liked being able to put a hunch together based on what she knew or what she was learning, about globalization, immigration, the melting pot or its failure, and she liked the mystery of not knowing the rest. There was no mystery in Minnesota. Everyone looked the same, you betcha, except the Indians, but that's another story.

One Friday at dusk Hector was walking up the avenue. He saw Helen waiting at a bus stop. She would think back to that day, and her decision, over and over again. Because she never waited for the bus, and rarely took the subway. She walked. She was a rain dog, in the Tom Waits spirit of that term, she said, after I'd introduced the class to Tom Waits. I taught a socio-history of music, and Helen was a foot soldier, even with a wad of cash in her pockets. No taxis for Helen, and often no buses. And the thirty something blocks back up to her dorm were a breeze, and an education, especially the crosstown blocks north of the park. She soaked up so much about New York on those walks. But that day, she could never remember why, maybe her spirits were low, she felt lonely, that day she elected to take it easy, take a bus, get a load off. And Hector came by. He spotted her. He said, hey, you look like you could use a drink. And Helen said she sure could. So he said, come on. I got a bottle, we'll take a nip on the drive. She said drive? Where? He said, come on, I show you how New York feels in a car. We take a drive to the Bronx. The Bronx. She'd never been to the Bronx. In New York three years and never been to the Bronx. Or Queens, or Staten Island. Not even Brooklyn. And she could count on one hand the times she'd gone lower than 14th Street. So, yeah, she thought, why not? An education, a threshold crossing, the real New York. The Bronx.

Hector drove a big old Plymouth, boxy as a sheet of plywood and twice as wide. He parked it on a street just outside a garage his brother Julio worked in. He got the keys from Julio, Julio shook his brother's hand, bumped shoulders, winked at the girl. And they were off.

They crossed the park at 96th, drove north on Amsterdam Avenue, windows down. It seemed like there was play in the steering wheel because he'd turn the wheel left to go left, and the car would stay straight until he turned it a couple of more times. A delayed reaction. (A gray area?) On the radio, salsa, or what sounded like salsa to Helen. They passed a bottle of Fundador brandy that went straight to Helen's stomach, and then her head. She'd skipped lunch, there was nothing there to soak up the alcohol, and she was getting such a great effect—that frisson she felt sometimes when Hector came into the shop and they kidded around, even flirted. He turned up the radio and encouraged her to sing, he encouraged her to let her hair fly in the wind. They flew right past Columbia, she turned to watch the buildings of the campus recede. North of Columbia was mythic, scary, and here she was, hair flying and brandy warming her guts. He turned onto 155th Street and now they were in the heart of Harlem and that created even more of a buzz, a buzz on top of the frisson, on top of the flirtation, on top of the brandy that was on top of the nothing that was in her stomach. We're not in Minnesota now, she thought. She felt so light-headed. She missed cars, she missed driving, she felt like she needed to get a car, or date a Hispanic guy who had one.

"Where are you from?" she asked Hector.

"Where ju think I fron?" he said.

"Ju not fron here," she said.

And Hector laughed.

"Ju right," he told her. He lifted the bottle of Fundador and filled his cheeks. He passed the bottle to Helen.

They crossed the Harlem River on the Macombs Dam Bridge. The Harlem River. The Macombs Dam Bridge. She didn't even know there was a dam, or a bridge, or even a river, and now she was crossing it and it finally felt like her life in New York was becoming a life in New York and not just another temporary exploitative stay at a privileged school. She would always remember these names when she recreated the story. The Harlem River. The Macombs Dam Bridge.

Now they were in the Bronx. Jerome Avenue, Mullaly Park, the Grand Concourse, East 170th Street. And she was laughing and singing and shifting in her seat with her elbows tight against her sides as if she was doing a little salsa and Hector told her, "Ju good," and she told him "Ju good, too." He said, "Ju so pretty," and she said, "but ju so old," and they both laughed. "I not so old for ju," Hector said. And Hector was right, wasn't he, she thought, because her boyfriend, the one who lived on the upper east side, the one she visited two or three nights a week, the one who couldn't see her tonight because he was seeing another girlfriend, he was even older than Hector. Or at least she thought he was—her boyfriend was forty-two, and Hector, maybe late thirties. She tried to put the thought of her forty-two-year-old boyfriend out with another girlfriend—*one* of his other girlfriends, or one of his *real* girlfriends because with Helen he never used the word girlfriend, he had a thing about the word girlfriend, it was too fixed in its associations and everything those associations required—she tried to put that prick out of her mind and just enjoy the Fundador and the wind and the street names and the music.

At 172nd Street near 3rd Avenue, Hector slowed down.

"Ah," he said, "an es-spot."

"Where are you going?" she asked him.

He needed to go upstairs and change, he said.

"Come," he told her. "I change, and then I take you for a drink."

She followed him to his building, a pre-war building of tan brick a couple of decades overdue for cleaning. Thick metal bars and sliding metal grates crosshatched the ground floor windows, out of which blared a confusion of salsa and thumping funky bass. The front door was ajar, the elevator broken, and graffiti, big black swirls of it that looked Arabic or Sanskrit, covered the walls of the staircase they climbed to the fifth floor. A heavy odor of insecticide hung in the hallways, she could taste it on her tongue.

"Ju out of breath," Hector said. "And see, I not breathing heavy at all."

She said, "You're used to it."

"I play football," Hector said. He pointed to his thick hairy calves. "These legs are the legs of a semi-pro."

Laughter as they continued to his door. Inside, he dropped his bag on the living room floor. The place was a mess of take-out plastic and empty bottles.

"Come," he said, "let me show you."

He led her into his bedroom. He swept his hands across the sheets and pulled the covers up toward the stained pillows. Dust balls gathered along the baseboards, and stacks of magazines scattered in disarray on the floor around his bed.

He removed his mailman shirt, pulled a tank-top over his head. He'd been in good shape once, she could tell from the lines of his musculature, but he'd gone a bit soft around the waist, the way all men do.

He unlaced his boots and tossed them on top of some magazines. He pulled off his socks.

"Hey," he said, "ju want I give you massage?"

And suddenly that seemed like a good idea. A complicated idea, but a good one. She needed to relax, and god, did she need some hands on her, hands that wanted to be on her and not on other girlfriends, too.

The disarray of the room—that didn't thrill her. Nor did its odor—a smell of soiled laundry left too long in a pile. But she felt that frisson and it was connected to a pulse that she could definitely feel accelerate in some compelling way. She remembered the first time she met Hector. He'd come into the shop, no customers were there, and she'd been feeling homesick, unable to concentrate, and for close to an hour she'd been stuck on the same page of a required text. Just the way he smiled when he handed her the mail bundle held together with a rubber hand, the goofy way he walked, and the incongruity of his blue shorts with the black stripe on a freezing gray December afternoon, all those things made her think, I'm going to like this guy. "What happened to the other girl?" he'd asked her. Helen said, "Fired," and Hector said, "I not surprised, she was so nasty." He said he used to be afraid to come into the store, he wanted to throw the mail the way paperboys toss the paper. "But with a smile like ju got," he told her, "I can tell I'n coming right up to the counter every day."

He unlaced her boots. Doc Martens. She kicked them off and lay face down on the bed. And his hands were so strong. The way his thumbs dug into the flesh around the spine, and the releases she got along the vertebrae, in the nerves of her shoulders leading down to her arms, at the ends of which her hands rest palm up and flaccid, almost like a drug had taken effect. He said I can't do you good with this on, and she pulled off her shirt. "And this too," he said, "in the way," and she unhooked the bra. "Mami," he said, "ju so beautiful," and he started to help her off with her skirt. And when he resumed the massage she could feel him, thick and hard and resting right in the center of her buttocks—a prelude she recognized because of her forty-two-year-old boyfriend and some of his proclivities, and she said you know maybe this is a bad idea and he said no no no mami, shhh, ju just relax, relax, let go all that tension, and he ran his hands around her shoulders and pinched the cords of muscles that linked her shoulders to her neck and he slid his fingers around her neck and rested them briefly on her esophagus, the tiniest pressure, maybe not even pressure, maybe not even the esophagus, but she picked up something, a signal, a warning, an intention, and he traveled a little further down until his hands were cupping her breasts and she did tell him no, and she did tell him stop and she didn't even know how or when he'd slid her panties aside and she didn't even know when or how he'd slid himself inside but there he was like all of a sudden, fat and thick and hard and hot and she pictured those thick hard muscular hairy calves and oh my god it was such a weird wild feeling and how could she ever deny that she was soaking wet but she was and he was in her and he drove himself up and in and home until she felt everything in him tense and she said no, not in me, but it was already too late, he was in deep, and then he was done, and his breathing slowed, and she could smell the Fundador brandy on his breath, hot on the dirty pillow. And then he relaxed. And he wasn't interested in any more massage and neither was she. She gathered her clothes and pulled them on and she said look, can you just take me to a subway, and he said he needed to sleep and she wasn't in the mood to argue. She pulled herself together, found his filthy toilet and pushed her fingers down her throat, scrubbed herself as much free of him as she could with her hand and his dirty soap, and wound her way back to the Grand Concourse where she found the D Train.

Later that night, she told me how she started crying when the train crossed back into Manhattan, and how foolish she felt when she thought about what she had just done, how naïve she had been, how lucky she was. She said, "Can I come over?" She said, "I know it's late and you were supposed to be out with someone else—are you even alone? I almost don't even care, I just want to see you. I need you to hold me."

And she came over. She burst into tears when she entered, and she cried when I put her in the shower, and she rested her head on my shoulder and cried when I got into the shower with her, and she dropped a hand around the erection I couldn't help getting, and I couldn't tell if she was crying anymore or if the shower was just getting in her eyes. But she could talk like she wasn't crying because she asked through the water in her eyes what I'd like to do, and I said, you know, whatever you're comfortable with, given the circumstances, you've been through a rough experience. (And I didn't remind her that just hours before, I'd been with another girl.)

We turned off the water and pulled back the shower curtain. She sat on the toilet and pulled me toward her and blew me perfectly with her hair soaking wet and the rivulets of water running off and dripping down the young large firm white breasts. And after, in the living room, wrapped in towels, she said she couldn't believe that she'd been raped. She wanted to know what I thought and I said, you know, I don't know, it sounds like there might be some gray area. She said, you don't think I was raped? I said I think whatever you think happened, happened, it's just, I don't know what you'd call it, at least in a courtroom, because even in your own version you went on your own volition, and you drank, and you flirted, and you got on his bed, and you took off your clothes. Anyone might get the wrong impression. But, I added, if you want, we'll go to the police station right now, we'll file a report.

"Not tonight," she said.

I said tomorrow is too late.

I gave her a twenty for a taxi, which I always did. Knowing full well she was just going to pocket it. She never took taxis, or even the subway. She was a rain dog.

I offered to walk her down, flag a taxi for her on the avenue. But she told me, no, she said I looked tired, and she was okay. Really.

All of that occurred to me, just from that sheet flapping in the wind. A sheet with a slogan. When I realized I'd reached my street, I thought, wow, I couldn't tell you how I just got here. Like I'd been in a kind of fugue state. And inside my apartment, I hesitated in the entrance where she had cried, and I stared into the bathroom. The shower, the toilet. The whole place felt chalked off and frozen like some crime scene. And it was as if Helen was still there, dripping. I could see her that clearly. And the part I knew for certain, the part that had no gray area, it was so black and white. Sometimes things are that clear, that black and white. Especially to young people. Maybe some older people, too, I don't know.

But I'm interested in what you think. Is it black and white to you, or do you think there's some gray area here? I mean, could you say for certain, one way or the other, if Helen was raped that night?

THE PERFECT THROW

You throw rocks or peaches or crab apples or anything you can get your hands around at squirrels or cats or blue jays or anything that can move, and some things that can't. You never think you'll actually hit the thing, whatever it is. You've missed the sides of parked trucks, you've missed houses. But today, when you release the fist-sized stone over the scrub oak lining the gully, you know instantly, from the arc, the velocity, the trajectory, that this time you have made the perfect throw, a strike, a basket, a bullseye. Your target will be hit, squarely, solidly, with lethal force. And your heart nearly stops, because this time your target is a person, a human being, damn near a next door neighbor who lives just four houses down the block and happens to be the younger brother of a kid in your class who's recently, you can't figure out when, recently become stronger than you, who's no longer afraid of you, who's actually held you between his arms in an unlocked bear hug and subdued you, squeezed the air out of you, made you not only stop, but say you'll stop so that there couldn't be any confusion about the nature of your absolute capitulation. You had to say it loud enough for him to hear, and the onlookers to hear, and the younger brother had been one of the onlookers. He watched dispassionately, the way a judge watches a hanging, and you would not forget that look, a look that said your surrender equals a broader justice.

The younger brother is named Karlsen, he works the Newsday newspaper route, he gets up early in the morning when not even the fathers of the block are awake, and he rides his bike with the two baskets on either side of the rear wheel filled with fresh papers standing vertically on their edges. You do not like Karlsen, you never have. You like his older brother even less, especially now that he is stronger than you. You don't like their family, neither do your own mother and father. They have said things about Karlsen's family. The father works at the lab, the mother works at the community college. They are boring people, reclusive, scowling, superior. They never say hello, they never say anything. And earlier this month, Karlsen got your German shepherd dog Wolf in trouble, because Wolf was jumping his fence every morning and lying in wait for Karlsen on his paper route, and when Karlsen would pass by on his newspaper laden, dork-basket adorned bike, Wolf would explode from his hiding spot beneath the drooping branches of your front yard's Japanese red maple, and he would snap at Karlsen's feet spinning around on his bike's pedals, and if Wolf missed the feet, he would go for the raccoon tail that Karlsen had won for being the best paperboy on Eastern Long Island, a prize Karlsen was proud of, and that he displayed from its place on the bike's rear fender. Wolf would lunge for that tail, he would grab it between his jaws, dig his teeth into its fake fur, then drag his paws into the bluestone gravel road, jerking his neck back, swinging his head side to side like a hammerhead, and spreading his paws wider and lower until slowly, steadily, inexorably, Karlsen's bike would grind to a stop. At which point Karlsen would drop the bike in panic and Wolf would lunge at him over the fallen rear wheel, and then a dance would ensue with Karlsen dashing left and right around the handlebars, around the rear wheel, and Wolf rushing and lunging and snapping, at Karlsen's arms, his pants, his butt, and Karlsen crying and blubbering and maybe managing a sob-choked yelp. "Help," he'd cry, "help." And a houselight might snap on, a light at the end of a driveway, a front door might open. Or a car would purr down the gravel. And Wolf would dash into the shadows, his efforts at putting Karlsen's mobility to rest forever frustrated once again.

You know all this because Karlsen came one day to your door with his raccoon tail in his hand, and he showed that shredded tail to your father. The tail used to be bushy and fluffy and striped like the fur of a healthy raccoon, he explained, but the tail he held up now looked like something pulled off the ass of a drowned rat. Long, thick, hairless, with dusty trails of saliva that fermented nearly rabid. Wolf got punished then. Wolf took a beating he never forgot, with Karlsen watching so the dog would associate the pain with the dispassionate face of Karlsen, who watched the blows without blinking and listened to the cries without smiling. And when your father was done beating the dog, with your help he sunk a concrete slab into a corner of the backyard, and he situated an upside-down U-hook into the center of that slab, and he got a chain with quarter-inch-thick links and he hooked Wolf to that chain with a padlock so that neither Wolf, nor you, could ever set him free. And when he found that you'd been trying to set Wolf free, when he found the gouges in the concrete slab that you'd dug there with the claws of a True Temper twenty ounce straight claw hammer, he punished you with a week's grounding. You could go to school and back, catechism and back, but outside of educational or religious obligations, you could not spend one second with one foot off the property. And your time on the property would be filled with chores, chores that prevented you from even making eye contact with

Wolf. But your father couldn't prove whether or not you'd honored that grounding unless you told him the truth, and you'd stopped telling your father the truth about anything since the beginning of fourth grade, and from the vantage point of halfway through fifth grade, that seems like a lifetime ago. So you wandered off the property, into the woods, along the gully, remembering how great it used to be to walk around with Wolf, how Wolf riveted the attention of everyone with how big and how smart and how beautiful and how strong he was. And that's when you spotted Karlsen in the gully, and that's when you found that rock, that big round heavy rock that fit so perfectly into your palm, like a baseball. And you let that rock go, and there it is, high in its arc and climbing so that when it makes its descent it will pick up murderous velocity and when it comes down it will slam pure and straight into Karlsen's right temple, right where the taped stem of his goddamn glasses fit behind his ear. You know the throw is so pure, so straight, so perfect, and you know the connection will be so fatal so instantly, that you don't even stick around to see your handiwork. You'd like to. You'd like to watch it hit, hear it thud, you'd like to see Karlsen's skull split open and the gloopy brain matter ooze, and you'd like to go down to the spasticating corpse and drop a good steaming piss right into his brain pan. But even before the rock descends you're off on your PF Flyers, you're running faster than you've ever run, you're running so your heart presses into your ribcage, you're running faster than even Wolf could run, and you're back in your yard with Wolf, because you're grounded, and you're doing your chores, with the rake and the broom, well before the whirr of the first siren.

THE MOTIVE FOR METAPHOR

What happened that day in his therapist's office still surprised Maris years later, years after he'd left therapy, years after his therapist had died.

Theo—he was on a first name basis with this therapist, unlike some of the others; Dr. Pine, for instance, that monumental asshole whom Maris had seen for close to six years and never once called by his first name, and neither had Dr. Pine used his, it was always "Mr. Dea," this, and "Dr. Pine" that, with his brown shoes and his Windsor-knotted ties— Theo had asked him to bring a poem into a session, a poem he might want to talk about, a poem that, for some reason, it didn't have to be clear, did something for him, "made him feel exposed" was how Theo put it, "made him feel wide open." Maris brought two copies of Wallace Stevens's "The Motive for Metaphor." He'd expected to deconstruct it, like in a graduate school seminar, parse its lines, uncover its influences, expose its codes. Theo declined his copy, and asked instead for Maris to read the poem aloud.

Maris hesitated. "I'll feel like I'm at an audition," he said.

"It's okay," Theo told him. "You already have the part."

This was New York, Theo worked with numerous actors, and he knew all about audition anxiety.

Maris took a breath. He set his elbows on his knees.

"*You like it under the trees in autumn*," he began, and already he could feel something happening, his throat thickening, his pulse hammering. "*Because everything is half dead.*" There he came to a stop—he could hardly breathe.

"I can't," he told Theo. His hands shook.

"It's okay," Theo assured him, "it's okay. Now continue, please."

And Maris tried. But something had a hold of him. It quickened, then robbed, his breath. He got through the first verse, and began the second.

"*You were happy in spring*," he read, "*With the half colors of quarter-things.*"

And at "quarter-things" he stopped. At "quarter-things" it was as if he'd been slugged in the gut, in the solar plexus, and he doubled over in sobs that wracked his body, sobs he couldn't control, that frightened him in their depth, that took his breath the way a sudden and long fall can, and you wonder not when you'll get it back but if. And when it returns it's a huge insucking gasp and you explode in sobs even more convulsively, even though you know the sobs are sucking the water from the shoreline, as it were, the way a tsunami drains a bay.

He saw Theo twice more after that and they never made any sense of the incident, at least not to Maris's satisfaction. Then Maris left the country to make a film, his first shoot abroad, in Laos, a low-budget indie feature directed by a woman with a reputation in the margins of the business and a star who'd once actually been a star. He was gone longer than he'd expected—the shoot was a nightmare of mishaps that prolonged everyone's stay well beyond their visas' allowance. When finally they wrapped, Maris decided to travel, first into Cambodia, then Thailand. He'd left half his luggage behind in Vientiane and he couldn't go back for it. It felt like he'd left half his life. It didn't feel bad to lose half his life. He felt both lighter and nearer to destitute.

Half his travel involved laundromats, or washerwomen beating his clothes. He started drinking again, beer at first, then local rice and palm wines as he sat on crates in a wife-beater, watching women with weathered skin wring out his soiled shirts. The wines aggravated his ulcer. One night in Bangkok, he helped a Swedish student who was getting mugged on a dark avenue alongside Lumpini Park. He traveled with her by train to Chiang Mai. They waited a week for visas to China. Her family was wealthy so she paid for everything, out of gratitude, she said. The Thai people were accustomed to seeing women like the Swedish student. But the Chinese stared at her as if they were seeing a vision, a visitation, a miracle. Some nights in bed, Maris looked at her that way, too—the length of her, the yellow radiance—in disbelief. He'd reached a point in his deterioration—a hardening of the destitution he'd cultivated for two decades—that elicited sympathy from beautiful young women. They found him intriguing, romantic, woebegone. He was a cross between Tom Waits and Gary Cooper. Since leaving America, he'd punched two new holes in his belt, and still his trousers sagged.

He spent his first two weeks back in New York staring at the phone. He'd wanted to call Theo to say, let's just have coffee or something. He'd wanted to say he was fine, that he was beyond therapy. But he knew he wasn't, even if he didn't know why. It wasn't as if he heard voices, or stared into the void, say, of his refrigerator, which he used as shelving for scripts. It was just this gnawing anxiety, and the burning of his ulcer that kept him always within ninety seconds of a toilet. It was autumn, everything half-dead. He received a card from the Swedish student. She wrote of rhapsodies under the stars that night on the Yellow Mountain. He had to struggle to come up with her name. She'd become a quarter-thing.

When at last he called, he was told of Theo's passing.

"Of AIDS?" Maris repeated, stunned.

"Complications similar to," the receptionist said, "but no one knows . . ."

Maris said, "Theo was gay?"

But he hung up even as the receptionist explained something that he couldn't hear.

It was immaterial. It was all immaterial.

He took a job as an understudy in an O'Neill play. He could always rely on something drunken or Irish. He renewed his guitar playing, restored the calluses on his fingertips. He thought about how much he'd loved Theo, how Theo had saved his life without writing a single prescription. He wondered what it meant to love a man so much. And was it reciprocated? Theo was actually younger than Maris by about three years—he found that out after Theo's passing. All along he'd thought Theo was at least ten years older. Choices can age you, Maris thought. Choices and responsibilities, two things Maris had scrupulously avoided.

One day he was playing guitar on a bench in Tompkins Square Park. "Rex's Blues." A red-haired woman approached him.

"That's Townes Van Zandt you're playing, isn't it?"

She had an Irish accent.

Six weeks later he moved to Los Angeles where the red-haired woman belonged to a repertory company that welcomed Maris. The New York edge, they told him, is what they'd been missing. Maris told them he was from Montana, which was half true, but he didn't remember which half. You reach an age, he told them, when the lies become the truth and the truth, it never mattered anyway, at least not as much as you thought it did.

Unofficially, he became the company's artistic director. The young actors wanted to know what he knew, which, they believed, was quite a lot. He told them about "The Motive for Metaphor," and on the basis of his story, the company scribe wrote up a one-act with the same title. It ran for six weeks to capacity houses and critical acclaim. Maris directed himself. One night, he saw Dr. Pine in the audience. On another, he could have sworn it was Theo. He remained in character until he believed he didn't have another tear left in him for as long as he'd live.

TONIGHT AND FOREVER

One night, while looking at menus in their favorite Thai restaurant, Professor Ketch's girlfriend Julia touched his arm and asked, "Ketch, why do you love me?"

Professor Ketch looked up over his glasses. He was hungry, and there was a movie to catch, and both those facts conspired to make him peevish, and his peevishness at times when he was hungry and there were films to catch was nothing new to Julia.

"I'm sorry, what?" he said.

Julia said, "I'm just asking. I'd like to know. How come, that's all?" Her smile was awkward, and weak.

Professor Ketch dropped his menu.

He said, "This again?"

"You've never given me an answer and I'm just asking," she said, patting his forearm reassuringly. "I mean, no big deal, I'd just like to know. It's my self-esteem issues, I guess."

Professor Ketch removed his glasses. "You know I've been waiting to see this film for over two years. You know I've got a conference next week, finals the week after. And now you want to start another marathon about the quality of my affections?"

"I'm not asking for a dissertation, Ketch, for Christ's sake, just a candid, heartfelt articulation. I mean why can't you do that?"

"Why can't you just judge me by my actions?" Professor Ketch said.

Julia said, "I do, and that's why I'm asking. I don't understand your actions."

Professor Ketch folded his glasses and slid them inside his jacket.

"All right," he said, pushing back in his chair. "Do you understand this action?"

Julia said, "What?"

He fished a twenty from his wallet and tossed it near her plate. "Enjoy your dinner."

"What are you doing?"

"I'm out of here."

"No," Julia told him. "Wait."

Professor Ketch waited. "Well," he said, his arms ready to lift himself from his chair.

Julia said, "Forget it."

"Forget what?"

"Forget I asked."

"Till when forget it?" Professor Ketch said. "Till when? The main course? Dessert? Forget it till when?"

"I won't ask you again," Julia said.

"*Tonight* you won't ask me again?"

"Tonight," Julia said. "And forever."

Professor Ketch pulled his seat back in. "Forever. That's what, a threat? An utterance of resignation and finality? Am I supposed to feel threatened, or guilty?"

Julia picked up her menu. "What are you having?" she said.

"I might go for the *plak num*."

"No," he said, "wait. This isn't finished."

"I said I won't ask you. Christ, I'm hungry. I thought you were hungry."

"I'm not eating until I know."

"Know what?" Julia asked.

"Do I love you?" Professor Ketch said. He leaned forward

and asked again, in lower, more confidential tones. "I want to hear what you think—do I love you?"

"That isn't what I asked."

"It's what I'm asking."

"I asked why do you love me, not do you love me. I know you love me, or at least I've heard you, I don't know, I wouldn't say articulate—"

"You wouldn't say articulate."

"—no, you haven't articulated. You've equivocated. You've rationalized."

"Rationalized?"

"Oh come on, you know what you do. You're the freaking professor with the five-dollar words and I'm the little chippy with the goo-goo eyes and the big dumb tits."

"You're the little what?"

"The chippy, the ex-student, the easy-ass little fuck bunny who lets you get away with whatever the fuck you want while you go off to conferences and fuck who knows how many other easy-ass little fuck bunnies."

"Ah, so that's what this is about."

Their waitress appeared, the one who usually served them. She was Thai with long black hair and soft brown skin and impeccable Buddhist humility and better English than she pretended. Professor Ketch imagined she was a graduate student, something like Julia, working part time, taking class part time, and sleeping her way to a PhD.

"We need more time," Professor Ketch told her.

Their waitress *wai*'d and offered a delicate bow, and Professor Ketch put his hands together and *wai*'d back.

"I hate when you do that," Julia said.

Professor Ketch caught and held her eye.

"There doesn't seem to be much about tonight that you do like, is there?"

"Okay, here we go. The professor flips the terms of the question. Look," she said, leaning forward. "I was your student, fucking eons ago."

"It's little more than two years, actually."

"Actually this," she said, holding up her middle finger. "And I'm not your student now."

"Ah, but there's so much you have to learn," Professor Ketch said, spreading his arms out wide.

"Maybe," Julia said, "but allow me as a friend to inform you: you ain't the teacher. You ain't even the TA and in my education I'm miles beyond what your ass can provide."

"Gosh, I love when you break into vernacular," he said. "There! There's something I love about you. *Dear Julia, I love when you break into vernacular. Love and oodles of kisses, Ketch.* Now can we fucking order so we can get to the movie on time?"

Professor Ketch signaled for the waitress.

"You don't get there on time, you get there forty-five minutes early and read a book."

"If you like, I'll give you your ticket and save you a seat, or am I guessing correctly that you'd rather sit by yourself tonight since you find me so repugnant."

"You're an asshole."

"And you're a crybaby little cunt."

The waitress appeared.

"I'm sorry," Professor Ketch told the waitress, "I was premature."

Julia said, "That's ironic."

The waitress *wai*'d again and slid away unperturbed.

"Ah," the professor said, "now we go after the swordsmanship."

Julia dropped her forehead into her hands and shook it.

"Baby, the day I don't do it for you in the sack, well, you know where to find the door. Unlike the slum you crawled out of, this city's bursting with young able studs, some of whom might—what is it you like?—articulate, is it?"

Julia said, "Stop."

"Stop?"

She raised her head. Her face was a mass of tears.

"Just please fucking quit it, please!"

"Hey, you keep your voice fucking *down*," Professor Ketch said anxiously.

"Oh fuck you!" she screamed. Standing, Julia swept her table setting into the Professor's, knocking his plate and his water glass into his lap. "Just fucking fucking fucking fuck you!" she said, running past tables for the door.

Professor Ketch stood, mortified, speechless, his lap running with water.

Their waitress stared.

Face, Professor Ketch knew, was important to a Thai, and losing it, publicly, with outbursts of anger, was damaging. Open-mouthed, he pointed toward the door and moved awkwardly in its direction.

The waitress *wai*'d.

An hour later, while he was fucking Julia, Professor Ketch noted that her lubricity was less than optimal. When it was optimal, when her vaginal walls were slick as 10-30 motor oil, he penetrated farther, beyond a trap door as it were, until his penis encountered a ridge, a soft-wet uterine under-cropping that angled his penis down even as his hips drove forward.

And when he hit that ridge he knew he'd hit a truth, a soft, wet, irrefutable truth, the kind that made Julia yelp, the kind that, in his discipline, was rare, was the grail, was alchemy.

Not finding that alchemy tonight, and sensing, through the less than optimal viscosity that he wouldn't, he rolled onto his back, pulling Julia on top of him, and allowed her to grind out some second best truth of her own. He loved to watch her in this position, loved to watch her put on her homegirl show. Taking her tits into her hands, sucking one, then the other, her thick thighs powerfully pumping her pelvic floor like a piston. Then swinging a one-eighty, lowering her forehead to the mattress and with manicured fingers separating the bubble cheeks of her ass. He took the small bedside flashlight and trained the beam on her anus while into its puckered rim she slid a red fingernail cuticle deep. When he cut the flashlight's beam, she knew it was time to spin back around and to cover his face with her tits, her miraculous tits. He buried his nose between them, shook his head from side to side, slavered over them and allowed himself to disappear into some primordial libidinal zone. His index finger circled her anus and coaxed her forward, then back, forward, then back, and from her chest came a low earthy grumble that grew into spastic full-throated screams that both delighted and infuriated him because to scream she needed space and that space pulled her tits away from his face and her anus off his finger. But she knew how quickly to resume the position, to re-smother his face and re-cover his finger, and when he thickened, when he was close, she knew how to pop off of him at exactly the last instant and to face-fall deeply over his cock and to bury his cock between her cheeks, and to pull the braids back from her face so that he could watch her concentrate and work to accommodate the jets of semen he bazooka'd onto her uvula, and she knew how to keep her mouth over his cock, to throat it back and forth and to linger at the head and to dive back down and to take it out and lick and teethe and tease its shaft and to tongue the pool at its tip and to smile around the cum-string connecting her lips to his dick and then to slide her tongue over that cum-string and swallow it and return for more, for whatever might be left, and then to kiss his prick, and his balls, and his thighs and calves and toes, and to run her fingertips like feathers up and down the length of his torso and legs and feet, and to not ask him about whether or not he loved her, or how he loved her, or why he loved her, not now, in bed, in the early hours of a night, with his semen still sliding toward her stomach and his penis against her lips and his eyelids falling heavily over his eyes, and the Thai dinner long forgotten and the movie probably just letting out and the salsa from a party one building over just beginning to filter in through the half-open window.

Thirty minutes later, Professor Ketch removed a Granny Smith apple from the refrigerator. He ran a perfunctory splash of water over its green surface, then bit into it, still wet, its hard sour taste pursing his cheeks.

He studied the reflection of his flat stomach in the hall mirror. His colleagues his age—early forties and older—had all softened and settled somewhat over their belts. Not Professor Ketch. He took another bite of the apple. These fights, he thought, and the sex after, and then the hour so late, the energy so low, leaving only time for an apple, they're what kept him in shape. Not a terribly high price to pay.

He took his seat in the living room and turned the TV onto C-SPAN. Julia joined him, curling her long thick-thighed legs under her on the futon. They watched the Senate confirmation hearings on Condoleezza Rice, and they listened to her lies and equivocations and utter naked falsehoods. And they watched the Senators accept her naked falsehoods without outrage or follow-up.

"Of them all she disgusts me the most," Julia said. "They must have run out of white white supremacists."

"This country," Professor Ketch said, shaking his head. "It's going to hell."

Julia said, "This country is hell and always was."

There was more to her statement than met the ear but at his age Professor Ketch knew better than to elicit what exactly that might be. He was tired, and he'd heard it all before, if not from Julia then from others. He'd probably even said it himself, once, when he was their age.

What he liked about Julia was how well she intuited things. He stood up, went to the bedroom, came out in his underwear and carrying a pair of shorts. Immediately, she began regrouping her things and pulling them on. She might ask a question or two now, about this filmmaker, that author, and those questions might have some associative energy connecting them to her earlier questions, but that energy would be easy enough for him to ignore while at the same time specific enough for him to offer her either an assurance or a warning in code. Something she couldn't quote and pin him down on some one dinner, two dinners later, but something nonetheless that they both understood.

Julia got fully dressed, he remained shirtless. He reached around her to the mantel and pulled a ten-dollar bill from his wallet.

"You're not going to walk me down?" she said.

"You don't mind," he said, "do you? It's still fairly early."

She said okay. She understood that that was the punishment for having brought up the question that would ruin the dinner and postpone the movie and she thought that, sure, okay, she could live with that punishment.

At the door he handed her the ten. "Make sure you show me the receipt," he told her.

It was a running joke. A cab to her place cost six dollars on a bad night. On a good night, a night, that is, when she left before midnight, she wouldn't even take a cab. Sometimes she walked, sometimes she took the bus or subway. And then, back in her room, she'd put the crumpled ten-spot on her desk and she'd look at it while she wrote entries in her journal or wrote e-mails to friends back home or wrote letters to Professor Ketch, long letters, letters that kept her awake sometimes till dawn, and she'd wonder about what that ten meant. Ten more than zero? Ten less than twenty? Ninety less than a hundred? Or none of those? Or all of those?

"Call me," she told him.

Professor Ketch said he would, of course.

She kissed him, and smiled, and turned, and stopped at the top of the stairs.

"Sorry," she said, her eyes glistening, "about earlier. Ruining the dinner and the movie and all."

Professor Ketch shrugged it off.

"I do know you love me."

Professor Ketch said that was good.

"Do you think the movie might come around again sometime soon?"

Professor Ketch turned his hands palms up. He covered his mouth, trying to stifle a yawn.

"I know," she said, "I should let you get to bed."

Professor Ketch agreed. It had been a long, draining day.

"Okay," she said, "call me."

Professor Ketch nodded.

"Oops," Julia smiled. "I already asked you that, didn't I?"

Professor Ketch told her don't worry about it.

Julia said, "Bye," and he watched as she popped down the steps.

He watched her descend, round the turn in the stairs, leave his sight. He listened as she walked toward the door, listened to her open the inner door, then the outer door. He didn't close his door, and lock it, and throw the bolt, until he heard the outer door draw closed.

He didn't know that sometimes she opened the inner and outer doors, and allowed them to close, but didn't pass through them. He didn't know that sometimes she tiptoed back up the stairs to his door and listened.

While he what? While he watched more C-SPAN? Or found a movie on cable? Or sent e-mails? Or made phone calls? Who, she sometimes wondered, would he be calling this late? Because she would take out her cell phone and look at its dark unlit face remain implacably dark and she knew it wasn't her. Sometimes she resisted the temptation to call him from her cell phone and find out.

AUTUMNAL

Her husband had slept with their daughter. Even years later that fact preceded her like a breeze, an odor both unpleasant and compelling like the smoke from a marijuana cigarette. When she entered a room, there were whispers and nods and glances, which she simultaneously ignored and assessed. She had learned how to exploit, even enjoy the enduring scandal, the speculation, the gossip. It aggrandized her, elevated her, separated her from the pack. It had happened when she still lived in Europe. She was thirty-seven then, her daughter fifteen.

Now she was in her mid-fifties, though she claimed early forties and often passed for it. She wore things that led attention away from details that disclosed age—the hands, the throat—and directed it to areas that recalled the ache of youth. Tonight, at a party given by the widow of a famous writer, her backless dress scooped down to the lowest lumbar, offering then withdrawing glimpses of her buttocks, depending on her posture and one's angle. The guests, male and female, even the caterers, lingered half-steps behind her, their eyes darting downward.

Her name was Eliza, Eliza Birtwistle, née Craven. In England, in her late twenties, she had married Lord Birtwistle, and though Lord Birtwistle had slept with their daughter, and then died several years later off in his wing of the castle, and though there had been several husbands since, she still used the title that that marriage had conferred.

In the summer of 1986, on Long Island's East End, Lady Birtwistle was the most photographed woman over thirty.

He was finalizing an early draft of the famous writer's authorized biography, and were it not for Lady Birtwistle's backless dress, his work would have been easy: all the principals gathered in one large house. He was tall, lanky, soon to be divorced. An academic, he'd made a name for himself writing the bios of tough guys. He was Irish, Pat Gildea, working class from Queens, but his accent was Philadelphia, it was Harvard, it was closer to Lady Birtwistle's, actually, who'd grown up in a hill station in India in the twilight of the Raj, than it was to the accents of his childhood. Geographically, she had come far from her childhood, but he, by the sound of it, had come farther. Apart from a rigid propriety, he was the perfect choice for the famous writer's biography: both had run, then hidden, from their pasts.

He would be dead in seven years, at sixty-four, and Lady Birtwistle would not be his last lover, but she would be his last love.

They were on a third-story balcony extending off the dead writer's studio. The moon had risen over the potato fields. Steam clouds hung over the blue-lit pool that people in their twenties splashed in without any clothes. She had been telling him about her days as a model in Paris, about intersecting with Kenneth Bray, the famous writer, and with the Kenneth Bray set. She alluded to an affair they may or may not have had; everybody was having affairs, everyone suspected them. She became fast friends with Victoria, the famous writer's wife. They lunched together, gambled on the horses, attended soirees thrown for visiting Black Panthers. It was all very Left Bank, she told him.

She omitted, the biographer in Gildea noted, any reference to her husband, but Gildea was at best only half-listening. He stood at an angle behind her, peering down over the rim of his wineglass. The hipline of her dress, just where the buttocks rose, alternately discovered then concealed what appeared to be a diamond-shaped birthmark.

"You can pull it back a bit if you like," Lady Birtwistle told him. She straightened her posture, her spine forming a perfect valley between the smooth hard slopes of her back. "The last one to check said there was nothing underneath."

He begged her pardon.

She took the fingers of his free hand and guided them to her coccyx just below the fabric of the dress. "I said pull it back."

His son, Douglas, was a problem. The boy would soon turn sixteen. He was curious, judgmental. He was fiercely loyal to his mother, who had recently introduced him to photography. He was in the process of developing a portfolio, as one was continuously reminded. His initial reticence around Lady Birtwistle changed to fascination. He filled rolls of film with her image: reading, applying makeup, waving away flies. What was it like, he wanted to know, to be a model during the Sixties?

"You know what they say, darling," she told him.

Douglas shook his head.

"If one remembers the Sixties, one wasn't there."

In preparation for his senior year he read Willa Cather and Scott Fitzgerald, but Lady Birtwistle insisted on giving him Henry Miller.

"I knew Miller, darling," she said.

"Miller," Gildea snorted. "Miller wasn't a writer." His nose curled as if at an unpleasant odor.

"Oh? And what was he, Professor," Lady B. said, sipping her wine, "in your vastly experienced and educated opinion?"

She appeared unflappable. Aside from the firm buttocks, it was the quality that had drawn him to her most. Now he experienced it more as an annoyance. They'd been sharing a beach house for three weeks. Douglas had come out at week two.

"At best," Gildea said, "a diarist."

Douglas said, "You keep a diary, don't you?"

Lady B. arched her eyebrows.

"That's hardly the point," Gildea told his son.

"What is the point, Professor?" Lady B. asked him. "I think Douglas should know and then Douglas, dear, would you come to the beach and explain it to me. I'm going for a swim."

She swallowed off the rest of her wine, stood, and dropped her wrap to the floor. Her thighs were thick, but hard, like the rest of her body. Like her head, Gildea thought. Like her heart. A Botticelli, but hard as a statue.

"I hate the way she says 'Professor,'" Gildea said. "As if it's some kind of curse."

Father and son watched her drop down into the dunes. Douglas gathered his camera and tripod and kit with lenses.

"Where are you going?" his father asked.

Douglas inspected the contents of his equipment bag. "Do we have any Henry Miller?" he asked.

"Certainly not," Gildea said, "but if you must read him we can find a copy, I'm sure."

Douglas said, "Where?"

Gildea pushed himself up from the patio chair. "In the gutter," he said.

Inside his study he was too distracted to work. He found his thoughts trailing to Lady B., to her diary habits. Did she keep one? and if so, what had she written about him? About them? The incest scandal that never appeared on her lips but whispered through everyone else's—how had she responded to that? That would be intriguing to discover.

Through a pair of field glasses that had come with the cottage Gildea checked on Lady B.'s whereabouts. He spotted her just out past the surf zone executing mechanically precise backstrokes. Douglas bent like a surveyor at the viewfinder of his camera, the legs of the tripod sunk into soft sand a foot or so into the tideline—not a safe place for a camera. Gildea resisted going down to the shore and cautioning Douglas; he'd have to learn for himself.

As Gildea had suspected, Lady B. carried no journal, no notebook, there didn't even appear to be an appointment book in her belongings. She was the busiest, most sought after woman Gildea had ever been involved with; she was also the least reflective. She maintained investment portfolios in London and New York. She owned nothing. She lived out of suitcases.

First there was the incest, then there was the acrimony, then the threats. She never carried out the threats, as Lord Birtwistle had predicted. You can get used to anything, he'd told her, and he was right. The incest hadn't lasted long. A year perhaps, no longer. Ingrid was institutionalized, there were rumors, and then Lord Birtwistle's premature death in suspicious circumstances. More rumors.

She moved in with an elderly Jewish man who appeared to be in robust health. He was obscenely wealthy, he sailed, he raised Giant Schnauzers. He promised her everything, boasted to company that Lady B. restored his youth. For two years she had nothing but anal intercourse. He left her nothing, not even a puppy.

The next one, the son of a famous Hollywood producer, left her everything. But everything wasn't a whole lot—there had been staggering medical bills, the man had been ill, then invalid. But it was enough to keep her in motion, then good company.

Gildea, she felt, was the silliest man she'd ever met.

"A man of six-foot-five," she reported to the famous writer's widow, "is supposed to cast a shadow, not be one."

"He's a biographer," Victoria Bray said. "That's his job."

They sat alongside the Bray pool drinking Bloody Marys at a round table below a Campari umbrella that one of Victoria Bray's daughter's friends had stolen from a sidewalk café.

"He's incapable of real insight," Lady B. said. "He's in awe of the fame and the money."

"Exactly," Victoria Bray said. "That's why we hired him."

"He's going to make us all look like a pack of dullards."

Victoria Bray said, "Good. We were."

Some mornings Gildea worked at the Brays'. Victoria Bray stood at the kitchen window looking out past the grape arbor into the yard, the drive, the woods, which her cats had turned into a graveyard for anything smaller than they. Nine thirty a.m., a tumbler of scotch or a snifter of cognac on the counter at her hand.

"For the wind," she would explain, although Gildea never asked.

"The wind?" he'd say.

"It affects my breathing." In front of her enormous chest she rolled her hand, suggesting a respiratory maelstrom in the pulmonary region.

Discreetly, Gildea glanced out into the windless yard—the scientist, the biographer in him. The oak and sycamore leaves hung leaden as ornaments under the blanket of East End August humidity. "Well," he said, pointing to the staircase leading to his work up in Kenneth Bray's studio.

"Yes," she told him. "Go work. Go understand us. Tell Grace if you need anything."

From the studio's balcony he'd watch the pool area fill up with the Bray house guests. The daughter and her friends, other local luminaries without pools. The ocean was less than a mile away. On the half hour Grace carried out a tray with ice and cans of beer and fresh glasses. She placed used glasses on the tray, emptied ash trays into the used glasses, and carried them back across the lawn, sweat shining on her dark skin. These were frivolous people, Gildea thought. They were lucky and careless. Is that what made them so appealing? Is that what drew him to Lady B.? Often he'd bring that conflict back with him to his own studio.

"This is wrong," Lady B. told him one morning, holding up a sheaf of his manuscript. She wore a towel around her waist and a bikini top. Her blond hair hung straight and wet at her shoulders.

Gildea lowered the glasses on his nose. "It's in progress," he told her, "it isn't wrong. And I've asked you not to look at it until I ask you." He took the papers from her hand and slid into his desk chair.

"Well I looked," she said.

"Okay, you looked. Please don't look anymore."

"Is this really what you're going to write?" she asked, leaning at his desk, riffling more pages of his manuscript, half the diamond shaped birthmark above her buttocks peeking out from the towel.

He tried to ignore her, the fresh clean scent of her. She took long aromatic baths following her morning walks, or swims, or yoga.

"Baby?" she said, her tone softened. She laid a hand on his shoulder.

"All right," he said, removing his glasses. He rolled back the desk chair and patted his lap. "Tell me what's wrong with it."

Lady B. looked toward the door. "Is Douglas here?" she asked.

One day at lunch Lady B. told him, "You write about tough guys."

Gildea waited. "And?" he said.

She blew out a cloud of smoke. She'd taken up smoking again that summer, she said to keep away the mosquitoes.

"And I find that rather piquant."

"Piquant," Gildea said.

"For a man . . . what is it you Americans say? For a man so in touch with his feminine."

Gildea shifted uneasily. As a boy he'd been called "Patsy." It drove him to take up boxing, and then books.

"I don't think that's true," he said.

"No," she told him, "it's true. Douglas, don't you think your father is in touch with his feminine?"

Douglas looked up from the *chaise longue*. He was reading *Tropic of Cancer*. "What choice does he have?" Douglas said.

"Marvelous," Lady B. said. She applauded. "Touché."

Douglas called his mother from the IGA in town. It made him feel disloyal to call from the beach house his father shared with Lady B.

"I know he's living with someone, Douglas, you don't have to lie for him."

A Schubert piano sonata blasted from the record player. Between that and the traffic, it was difficult for Douglas to hear. But since the troubles between his mother and father, it wasn't really necessary for him to hear his mother's words. He just needed to be on the other end.

"I'm not lying," Douglas said.

"You're not lying?" his mother said. "You're not telling the truth."

He pictured her sprawled on the couch in the living room, the blinds dropped against the afternoon, the TV on mute, her hand dangling against a chilled bucket of white wine on the carpet, the ashtray on the coffee table spilling butts. It hurt him to compare this image in his mind's eye with the ones he retained of Lady B., who was actually a bit older than his mother. "What is it that she does?" he'd asked his father, when he'd found Lady B. becoming a fixture in his own imagination. "Eliza?" his father said. "Eliza is the answer to the question." "What question?" Douglas wanted to know, and his father said, "Ah," nothing more. Douglas pictured how delighted his mother would be if she could see what a fool his father had been reduced to by Lady B., what a slobbering puppy, what a pathetic get.

"There's just the two of us, Mom, I told you."

Lady B. came out from the IGA. Douglas felt his heart—he was falling in love. What had she meant, he wondered, recommending Henry Miller? And the incest rumors—she had seen everything, she was capable of anything. Lady B. pointed to the car and a black teenager in a red apron wheeled a grocery cart past the phone booths over to the car's trunk.

"Just the two of you," Douglas's mother said, "and what whore?"

"Don't call her—" Douglas said, then caught himself.

His mother told him to enjoy the rest of his vacation.

Douglas returned to the city six days later, on his sixteenth birthday. His father had given him an annotated edition of *A Portrait of the Artist as a Young Man*, Lady B. gave him an album of photographs by Man Ray. They promised to visit him in the fall.

That November, Douglas had a showing of his photographs at a campus studio. "Tropic of Campus," he called it, and it had been written up in the local newspaper and treated like an event of artistic magnitude by the school's own journal. The school paper declined, however, to print any of the most representative photographs, the bulk of which were nude self-portraits.

Gildea and Lady Birtwistle were living in Sag Harbor by then. They traveled by ferry to Shelter Island, then Orient, then over to New London where they drove north to Douglas's school. They had reached a point of petty squabbling. Territory had already been staked, but the habit of bickering sustained. He argued for the symphonies of Sibelius on the drive, she wanted to hear the Beatles. The season had been late in changing, the trees were still a riot of color.

Gildea gestured toward the cassette deck. "Dear Prudence" was playing. "I don't see why we're listening to this, this *music*," he sneered. "It has nothing to do with the season, with us, nothing to do with autumn at all."

"Yes, Professor, yes," Lady B. said, "and you are nothing but autumnal, isn't that true?"

They checked into a B&B that Gildea found quaint and she squalid. She hired a taxi and told Gildea she would call from a pub. Two hours later he found her in a bar called Smitty's, a strip mall dive alongside a pizza place. Smitty's stunk of thick smoke and damp flannel. Douglas and his roommate were teaching Lady B. to shoot pool. Leaning over to take her shot, more than half her breasts fell exposed. On a nearby table was a pitcher of beer and three glasses. Douglas was smoking.

Lady B. looked up from her pool stick. "The Professor, boys. Look like you're not having fun."

The boys laughed nervously. Douglas dropped his cigarette and said hi. He introduced his roommate, Gavin. Then the three of them snickered.

Gildea ordered himself a scotch and water. From the bar he pointed to Douglas. "That's my son," he told the bartender. "He's sixteen."

"Sixteen?" the bartender said. He looked like a recently retired cop—the lumberjack forearms, the hard spread of his gut, the mustache an idea, an experiment he probably still heard jokes about. "But his mother—"

Gildea cut him off. "That," Gildea said, "is not his mother."

The bartender squinted at the pool table. "Got you, chief," he said, nodding slowly. "You want him out of here now?"

"I'll take care of it," Gildea said.

The bartender promised it wouldn't happen again. He held up a hand when Gildea reached for his wallet. "On me, big guy," he said.

It was Douglas's shot, an easy one, but he scratched. Gavin laughed. Lady B. sang along with the jukebox. "*Giant steps are what you take . . .*"

Douglas's show hung on temporary walls angled into a corridor outside the art studios. It was divided between black-and-white self-portraits in which his body was contorted into various cramped shapes, as if he were stuck in a box, the muscles in his arms and legs and torso straining against imaginary confines. Gildea found these surprisingly artistic. They disturbed him. He wasn't comfortable with the idea of his son as a sexual being, and these were photographs of a sexual being. Perhaps it was the undisclosed nature of that sexuality that disturbed him. There was something amiss in them, something queer.

The color shots were abstracts—nudes like Stieglitz nudes, Weston nudes, Man Ray nudes. Some included Douglas, or parts of Douglas, but most used an unidentifiable model, a woman. The valleys between breasts and ribcage, the crevice of the pelvis as one leg curled over another. A hand held palm out against a pair of buttocks.

These Gildea found inappropriate for a preparatory school exhibit. They were of the "Look, Ma, I'm taking photography" school. Some men might consider them graphic support of a son's masculinity, Gildea found them discomfitingly exhibitionist. Even perverse. The facelessness of them, the abstraction. These impressions were just forming when Gildea recognized a diamond-shaped birthmark on the model's buttocks.

Over a year passed before Douglas spoke again to his father. And Gildea kept all their interactions from then on strictly business. He offered advice on colleges, then graduate schools, but he was more like a guidance counselor obligated to perform an unpleasant function; there were other students he cared for more. Douglas understood that he had done irreparable damage. Lady B. was never mentioned.

Lady B. herself called Douglas the day after the exhibition.

"I could have had your father arrested," she told him.

Back at the B&B, after Gildea had dragged her from Douglas's campus by the wrist, leaving behind her coat, she had called him a middle-class boor, and he had slapped her, resoundingly. Then slapped her again.

"Darling," she told Douglas, "you wouldn't have known the man had such strength. I saw stars."

She needed Douglas to bring her her coat—she couldn't very well visit his school with a bruised face.

At brunch she ordered champagne. Douglas thought he might get one more afternoon with her, but she refused. "I can't go back there, darling," she said. "Not after what he said."

She ordered a second bottle. She wasn't making sense. His father may have made some public declamation about the incest, Douglas couldn't be sure. But in his father's biography of the famous writer, published two years later, Lady B. is referred to only as a fashion model from the early Sixties whose husband had slept with their daughter. He had utterly reduced her to that fact. Victoria Bray, the famous writer's widow, had raised no serious objections. She'd fought fiercely, however, over Gildea's characterization of her and her husband as alcoholic. That, she insisted, was a gross misrepresentation of their habitual drunkenness. "I ran a *salon*," she'd said, "not a saloon." Neither Gildea, nor his editor, could be moved. The misrepresentation stood—exactly the kind of misrepresentation Lady B. had been expected to prevent. Lady B. had failed her. Their friendship was seriously affected.

The only woman at Gildea's funeral was a secretary he'd had at Princeton the sixteen years he'd taught there, the four years he'd been Chair of Non-Fiction Studies in a graduate writing program. She was a plain woman, Douglas thought, the kind of plain woman who forms friendships with plain people in order to be seen on occasion in public having friendships. Douglas drove her back to the campus following the brief service.

"Your father was a well-loved man," she told Douglas at the pub she and Gildea used to stop in for cheeseburgers and a pitcher of beer. She picked at a plate of soggy French fries and sipped at a dark draft. "Ask anyone from that time," she said, "they'll tell you."

SNOW JOB

Gus Sztorc backed his 1982 Monte Carlo into a space near Macy's at the Smith Haven Shopping Mall. He was nibbling chocolates from a Whitman Sampler someone had left at the house on Christmas Eve—a re-gift: two of the chocolates were missing. From the back seat, his two little dogs, a poodle and a schnauzer, observed his motions, anticipating the opportunity to lick his sticky fingers. He nudged the bumper of the car behind him, pulled a few inches forward, and cut the engine. The dogs sat up, excited. "Not yet," he told them. He split another chocolate in two and tossed a piece to each. He licked his own fingers this time, and got out of the car.

His desert boots sunk into snow four inches deep. The white Christmas the weatherman had promised arrived a day late, but with fury. It was coming down over an inch an hour. The roads were hazardous, but that hadn't stopped the shoppers—the day after Christmas was the biggest sale day of the year. Only Gus Sztorc didn't go to the Smith Haven Mall to shop for sales. He went to experience one of the two things left in life that he still enjoyed: watching people be people—that is, phonies, hypocrites, con men, and petty thieves. They never let him down.

He popped the trunk and removed a box the size of a large suitcase. The box was wrapped with festive holiday paper depicting ice skaters and snowmen alongside green trees covered with brightly colored ornaments. The paper fit on the box like paint, its ends taped down tight as hospital corners without a wrinkle on the entire surface. Bright red ribbon circled the box diagonally at either end. Near the top, the ribbon's ends came to a bow—practically a work of art, floral art, a silky red dahlia on a flat-raked bed of bright paper. He closed the trunk. The dogs peered through the back window, but neither could see him. The poodle was near blind, and the window had fogged over. Both dogs began to whine.

"Yeah, yeah," Gus Sztorc said, trying to convince himself that the dog's cries didn't pierce his heart. The dogs were the other thing Gus Sztorc still enjoyed. They *owned* him—he let them do just about whatever they wanted, and he couldn't bear to deny them anything. Since his retirement six months earlier, his greatest joy was to put on a stack of Jerry Vale records, lie down on the living room floor, and have each dog fall asleep on his chest. Already each had had three chocolates from the sampler, though he knew they'd have diarrhea before he got them home.

With the gift-wrapped box under his arm, he walked into the lane toward the Macy's entrance of the mall, carefully placing his shoes into the steps others had left in the snow. Scores of shoppers bent into the snow and rushed past him as if they were in a race, a competition, as if a hundred people had arrived for a smorgasbord set for ninety-nine, and they were going to make good and sure Gus Sztorc was the loser. The empty plate. The booby prize. Wait till they found out, he thought, smiling. Wait till one of them claimed the booby prize in this box.

A "Leave-it-to-Beaver" type family approached, Mister and Mrs., Junior, and Sis, their arms filled with bags and boxes.

"Merry Christmas," Mister said to Gus Sztorc.

Junior corrected him. "Christmas is over, Dad."

"So it is," Mister agreed, winking at Gus Sztorc.

Sis said, "Happy New Year.

Gus Sztorc said, "Yeah, sure."

Other shoppers passed—mothers shouting at kids, fathers shouting at mothers, kids shouting at nothing. The kids slid, packed snow in their hands and threw it at parked cars and each other. They fell into the snow and made what might have been snow angels if anyone could see through the snowfall. Gus Sztorc was glad to be beyond it all—the kids, the gifts, Christmas. He hated all the holidays, but Christmas was the worst. The most phony, the most costly, the most disappointing. In his whole life, he couldn't remember receiving a single gift he truly valued, except the opportunity to nap with his dogs. The rest was bullshit and money. Everyone knew it, but everyone pretended otherwise. "Oh, you shouldn't have." "Oh, it's so thoughtful." Oh, up your ass, Gus Sztorc thought.

Ahead on the sidewalk, just outside the side entrance to Chess King clothing boutique, a group of teenagers loitered. They were all underdressed—unzipped denim vests, studded leather jackets, sneakers, and no gloves. They smoked cigarettes and shivered, pimples underneath their soft whiskers. Their hair looked like it had been hacked with hedge clippers, then slept on. Why, Gus Sztorc wondered, would anyone want to raise kids today? At least when he had his kids, he had no idea that they'd turn into pukes. They could, of course, and they did, but that hadn't seemed a sure thing. Today, you were either a Kennedy, in which case your kids would wind up news anchors or Congressmen or the leader of some charity in Africa, or you were a nobody, your kids pukes. These kids weren't Kennedys.

The unmistakable smell of marijuana drifted his way. The

kid with the joint at his lips sucked a long hissing inhale that puffed out the chest of his t-shirt. Gus Sztorc recalled a day fifteen, sixteen years earlier. He'd parked his car at Port Jefferson Harbor for a nap when he saw Chet, his own kid, fourteen years old, sucking a joint in the midst of a crowd like this. He looked like the embodiment of a nightmare, and from that moment on Gus Sztorc avoided contact with him. Maybe he shouldn't have, maybe he could have helped . . . but it was painful just to look at his stoned puss.

The kid with the joint exhaled.

He said, "What are you looking at, Fat Fuck?"

Gus Sztorc recoiled—he hadn't realized he was staring.

"Sorry, sonny," he said, shaking his head. "Merry Christmas."

"Hey," the kid said, cupping his crotch, "sonny this."

The other teenagers laughed. "Sorry, sonny," they shouted. "Merry Christmas, sonny."

Gus Sztorc moved on. To himself, he counted one, two, and a snowball caught him square between the shoulders. Another two flew past. A fourth caught him the leg.

Pukes, he thought. Complete pukes.

At the mall's entrance, he stomped the snow off his shoes. Then, to complete the show, he mimed someone just realizing they'd forgotten something. He tapped his trousers, he stuck his hands into coat pockets. It was all a bit unnecessary—no one was looking, but he liked to pretend they were, just in case. He liked everything to be perfect. Then, shaking his head as if he couldn't believe what a putz he was, he started back in the direction of his car, taking care to avoid the teenagers. If they saw him, they'd start again for sure. Tactically, ignoring the snowballs was a mistake, an invitation for more, and worse. Ten years earlier, he would have walked right up to the biggest puke and broken his nose. But he didn't go to the mall to fight pukes. He was done fighting pukes. And the well-wrapped box in his arms reminded him, he'd come here to do something else entirely.

He squeezed between a pair of cars and turned back into his own lane. Snow crept over the tops of his desert boots. He could feel it melting on his socks. He anticipated getting back into the Monte Carlo, turning on the floor heat, and getting the poodle onto the floor mat to lick his toes. As he neared the Monte Carlo, he swept the parking lot in all directions, making sure he was unobserved. Directly opposite his car were a large Buick and a small Toyota, each covered with snow, each parked front end first. He set the gaily-wrapped box down in the snow and leaned it against the Buick's rear bumper. Satisfied that he'd remained undetected, he crossed the lane and returned to his Monte Carlo, where the dogs waited behind fogged windows.

He got behind the wheel, tapped the front seat for the dogs, and started the car. He set the heat on high, blasted defrost, turned the windshield wipers on low. He pulled the desert boots from his feet and set them under the floor heat vents, he draped his socks over a vent on the passenger-side dash. The poodle got on the floor between his feet and licked his toes.

"Atta girl," he said, laughing against the initially tickling sensation. "Atta girl."

The schnauzer settled into his lap. And Gus Sztorc settled back for the show.

When Gus Sztorc retired, six months earlier, he'd canceled garbage collection and began taking care of the trash himself. At first he just collected it into a large lawn-leaf bag and tossed it into dumpsters he found behind strip malls or 7-Elevens or at the ends of the drives of local schools. He did a rotation of locations, always making sure not to visit the same place twice in a week, and always making certain to separate out trash that might identify him or his wife. That trash went into the fireplace where he incinerated it once a week. The other trash went out into the world. He found the routine relaxing and refreshing. It took him to new places, offered him new views, gave him something to think about. Like how were the dumpsters of Mastic-Shirley different from the dumpsters of Rocky Point? He got kind of a thrill out of dumping the trash like this. He felt like he was catching a break.

Before long, it started to seem like just another dull pain-in-the-ass routine in the land of cookie cutter developments and parking lots. That's when he hit on the idea of re-gifting. The first few times, he placed the trash neatly in a brown paper grocery bag from Waldbaum's or the A&P. He folded the top of the bag down neatly in two sharp creases. Then he drove to the supermarket, parked near the entrance, and left the bag in a cart where it might appear as if an absent-minded shopper forgot to trunk the final bag. Sometimes he leaned up against the line of shopping carts, sometimes he stood outside the entrance and dropped coins into one of the gewgaw machines. Sometimes he went back to the Monte Carlo. But each time he got the same result. A shopper would spot the bag, look around, look around again. Maybe they'd check their pockets for something. Maybe they'd retrace their steps a yard or two. Then, if they had bags, they might place their bags alongside the bag of garbage in the cart, and they'd wheel the cart off to their car and load the bags into the trunk or the back seat. Sometimes Gus Sztorc would start his car and follow them, and when they opened the prize and saw the mess, he might give a toot on the horn and a wave. Hey, neighbor, he seemed to say. Up your venal ass. And the woman or the man with the bag would wave back, awkwardly, not quite knowing if Gus Sztorc was Mr. Friendly Neighbor, or if he was the asshole who'd set them up. And Gus Sztorc loved it—the looks on their faces, and the universality of human idiocy, and human greed. Young and old, male and female. He wasn't learning anything new, but he was learning what he already knew better. Everybody was a puke. Once he saw one of his wife's friends, the wife of a local politician, walk off with a week's worth of kitty litter. Once he watched a pair of nuns stuff a lawn bag into the trunk of their car as if they were hiding a body. When he saw the nuns, he thought someone was playing a joke on him. Sometimes he'd drive to the nearest Friendly's. He'd get himself a cone, and each dog a scoop in a little bowl. God, people made him feel good.

Soon he learned that the bigger the bag, or box, the more anxious the shopper. Sometimes he'd leave three bags in a cart. Sometimes he'd tape up a box. Sometimes he'd find a large box in someone else's garbage, and he'd bring that home and fill it up, then go leave it somewhere and watch the charade.

The lead-up to Christmas had been particularly entertaining. Then, of course, people were accustomed to seeing others carry too many boxes, some of them wrapped in gaudy festive paper. He filled little boxes, big boxes. He wrapped them with bright foil, and patterned scenes, and sometimes with just plain brown paper. It was his instinct to mix it up, keep under the radar, avoid repetition, and always be plausible. He'd never in his life purchased wrapping paper, but this Christmas he had four varieties of paper, a bag of bows, two spools of ribbon, a new set of paper scissors and a roll of Scotch tape with a snowman and a reindeer pulling a sled on its body.

Today's package was the *coup de grace*, the *piece de resistance*, the *crème de la* fucking *crème*, if he could get French about it. This one packaged all the wrappers, all the bows, all the cards (with the names crossed out) and all the tinsel from all the meaningless gifts that had been exchanged over the previous two days—excluding the Whitman Sampler, whose chocolates remained good if compromised. There were the gifts from his two sons—a shirt too small, a shirt too big. He pissed on the big shirt, wiped his dogs' asses with the small—those went in. The gifts from his in-laws—a tie that looked like it was cut out of a shower curtain, a shower curtain that looked like it had been the wrapper on someone else's gift, a robe, a toilet kit—these he doused with barbecue sauce and lighter fluid and rolled them into a bag that he wrapped with foil. The gifts from his wife—a card without his name or hers, and a book about famous battles of the U.S. Navy (The fucking Navy! He'd been a Marine) . . . the card he signed, "To Ethel, from Julius" and lit it on fire; the book he'd cut out the inner pages and instead of inserting a water pistol, he'd shoveled up a few hard dog turds from his backyard and closed the book on them. He set all this into the box that had come with the gift his sons had given their mother, Samsonite luggage that must have fallen off a truck and had about as much utility for his wife as tits on a nun. To that mess, he added the past several days' debris: chicken bones, the heels and waxes from cheese, cracker boxes, broken ornaments, tissues, napkins, plate scrapings, turkey bones, chicken gizzards, stale bread, burnt lasagna, half-chewed meatballs, pie tins, cupcake wrappers, soup cans, empty milk cartons, half-a-week's kitty litter, and the bows and ribbons and cards and wrapping paper from the gifts passed around yesterday after dinner. For good measure he threw in the watch he'd received for thirty years retirement, a gold-tone Jules Jurgensen with a twist-o-flex band, water resistant to ten meters, that fogged up and stopped the first time he wore it in the shower—a piece of crap. Like his job, his sons, his life. And that's what he felt about Christmas, a piece of crap—a holiday when garbage got wrapped up and recycled and presented as gifts to hapless suckers who oohed and aahed at it, then returned it or gave it away to some other loser.

He wrapped the box carefully in the garage, his sons and his wife shaking their heads. And now he was sitting back, waiting to enjoy the fruits of his labor. And when he thought about it, days later, when the smoke had cleared and the snow had been plowed, he knew he shouldn't have been surprised. It had been building—what people will do when they spot a freebie, something for nothing, something they don't have to work for, something they can just take.

Two women spotted the box at the same time. One came from the shops, her arms full. The other came from her car, she was just heading in. She had two boys who ran in the snow in front of her. Gus Sztorc saw the boys first, or rather his schnauzer did, and she started barking. Gus Sztorc shushed her, and she curled back down on the seat beside him, her throat grumbling until his fingers tickled her calm.

Then the women converged, and Gus Sztorc couldn't hear what they said, but he could imagine. "That's my box." "You're full of shit." "Well it's not your box." "It is now." "No it's not." "Yes it is." Back and forth like that. Each with a hand on the ribbon, pulling this way, pulling that.

Someone, Gus Sztorc thought, is going to get hurt if this keeps up much longer.

So he honked the horn. Both women jumped, startled. The woman with the bags lost her grip, and her feet seemed to shoot straight out from below her hips. She fell straight back, flat as a plank. Then the dull thunk of her skull hitting the Buick's bumper. The other woman covered her mouth with her hand. She screamed for her boys to come back. She turned and ran. She didn't forget to take the box.

Gus Sztorc jumped out of the car and rushed toward the fallen woman. His bare feet in the snow sent his mind hurtling back to Korea. So did the blood, the helmet-like puddle seeping into the snow around the woman's head. He slid his fingers under her scarf and felt for a pulse—he pressed on one side, the other, nothing. A pair of headlights glowed blurrily at the end of the lane—then they started coming his way. He straightened up, hopped back to the Monte Carlo. The oncoming car slowed, and Gus Sztorc slid below the wheel.

Lonnie Lonigan sat in a booth of the Good Steer Inn on Jericho Turnpike. A True Blue curled smoke from his lip. He hated True Blue—the smoke was so thin he barely squinted. But his Lucky Strikes make him hack like he had a pint of pus in each lung.

On the wall at his elbow was a personal jukebox. He flipped through the offerings looking for the Italian love songs that gave Gus Sztorc such a kick. They'd both married Italian girls from the Bushwick neighborhood. Lonigan got stuck with a mutt. Janet Scaturo—one pregnancy and she pooched out. Two, she pigged. By the time she divorced him, she was pulling a caboose wider than a Volkswagen bus. Gus Sztorc got Lisa Accioli, pick of the Bushwick litter. A pain in the ass, worse than a Jewish princess, but two kids didn't blow her figure, and she held on to her looks, more or less. Even back then, eighteen, nineteen years old, she knew how to lick an Italian ice. It should have been the two of them, Lonnie always thought, but Korea, all the rest, shit got mixed up. Now all he cared about was the dirty movies. Was there a greaseball song about that? He punched in "Amore, scusami," "Mala Femmena," and "Addio, mi' amore." These days, three was all you got for fifty cents. There's your morning in America.

With his sleeve he wiped off a clear spot in the window. All he could see was snow, thick fat flakes of it. Headlights glowed on traffic slowed to a crawl. Gus Sztorc was ten minutes late, but that was okay. No rush. The plan was a lunch, a few beers, and Gus Sztorc would go home to the wife he couldn't stand, and Lonnie would pick up a six-pack and go to the dirty movies—the second best thing about being divorced. For the holidays, the Rocky Point Adult Cinema featured all the skins nominated for the Adult Video Awards. And every day they drew stubs for a free first-class flight out to Vegas for a stage-side table at the ceremony. Ginger Lynn, Nikki Charm, Christy Canyon—the winner got to sit with them all, three nights, in the flesh. And since seeing this year's *New Wave Hookers*, Lonnie had become obsessed. Every time he closed his eyes he saw Traci Lords doing very interesting things. It was going to take more than a blizzard to keep Lonnie Lonigan away from a crack at that freebie. And he had to win—Janet had cleaned him out of anything of any value.

He'd thought of asking Gus Sztorc for a loan—he knew his friend could spot him. But there was a funny thing about Gus Sztorc: he didn't approve of the skins. Even in Korea, when they were twenty, twenty-one years old. He wouldn't go along to the brothels. He wouldn't look at the magazines. The guys both hated him and respected him for it. And Lonigan learned it was best just to avoid the topic.

Outside a Suffolk County Police patrol car crept by, blue light flashing, the siren muffled in the snow. Then another cop car. And another. An ambulance followed. Lonigan shook his head—he'd driven a jeep at the Frozen Choisin, snow up to his kneecaps, and the only accident he had was pissing his pants when a bomb blew his jeep into the drifts. This snow—he could drive it drunk, he could drive it blindfolded.

Gus Sztorc couldn't. Lonigan saw him pull into the diner's lot, watched him slide and fishtail, then try to wedge into the space close to the entrance.

"Slow, you dumb bastard," Lonigan muttered.

Gus Sztorc spun his wheels again and again, and gave up. He motored over to a wide-open area in the lot's far corner. He lingered outside the car, saying goodbye to that blind goddamn poodle. The guy, Lonnie thought, was becoming a crackpot. When he came through the door near the register, his hair and beard glistened with snow.

"Gus, you fat bastard," Lonnie said, "I thought I was going to have to come out and park for you."

Gus Sztorc fell into the booth. He tried to speak, then choked back a sob.

Lonnie jumped up. He waved off the waitress. He threw his arm around his friend and told him, "Okay, Gussie, okay. Whatever it is, you hear me? Okay."

Lonigan knew all about his tricks with the garbage. Sometimes they went together, drank quarts of Schaefer and watched the show. But this one went haywire. His friend had crossed a line. He'd made himself vulnerable. Shit could happen.

When Gus Sztorc finished, Lonigan returned to his side of the booth.

"Look," he said, "it's two ways. Either she's dead and you did the right thing, 'cause no use getting fucked for something not your fault. Or she's not dead, which case someone finds her, they call the cops, she's all right. You keep your name out of it." He sat back and put a match to a True. "I'd rather get the cancer," he said, "than smoke these goddamn things. I gotta suck twice to get half a puff."

"Can we keep the focus here?"

"I'm saying, Gus, you got nothing to worry about."

"She had no pulse, Lonnie, did you hear me?"

"Yeah, I heard you."

"The woman died."

"That we don't know."

"What do you mean, we don't know?" Gus Sztorc said. "Were you there? Did you feel her?"

"Let me ask you something, are you a doctor?"

"She had no pulse."

"Oh, so you are a doctor. Maybe you could have a look at these hemorrhoids?"

"She didn't have a pulse, Lonnie."

"You didn't *feel* a pulse. You, a retired schmuck used to climb poles for the lighting company. You don't know a pulse from a putz, my friend."

Gus Sztorc smiled weakly.

"I know a putz," he said.

"I'm a putz, I know. But seriously, Gus—nothing. All right?"

"How do you figure?"

"Nothing legal, I'm saying. Spiritual, that's between you and *Il Papa*."

"It's not the pope I'm worried about."

"Look, legal—they got dick. Two women fighting over a box not even theirs. Freaking blizzard, no one sees past their nose. One falls, cracks her skull."

"And they call that manslaughter, Lonnie."

"No fucking way."

Lonnie Lonigan signaled for the waitress. She brought two schooners of Pabst.

"Remember," Lonigan said, "my brother-in-law's on the Suffolk County force. I'll give him a call, see what they have, careful like . . ."

Gus Sztorc said, "You talking about Jimmy?"

Lonnie said, "So?"

"The one you broke his nose?"

"That's a long time ago."

"The one I held him, arms back."

"Hey," Lonnie said, sitting forward, "the son of a bitch deserved it, number one."

"Number two, he hates my guts. You don't tell him shit about what happened."

"I didn't say tell, I said find out, all right?"

"What are you gonna tell?"

"Hey Gus, let me handle this, all right? You do the garbage and the dog-walking, yeah? And let me handle the cops and the skins, *capiche*?"

"The guy's an asshole," Gus Sztorc said.

"So he's an asshole. Who isn't? Now come on, finish your beer. Then we get a pint and a six-pack and go to the dirty movie festival."

Gus Sztorc shot him a look.

"These broads today, Gus," Lonnie said. "You heard of Nikki Charm?"

"What is she?" Gus Sztorc said. "Eleven?"

"They're all legal, Gus. Strictly professional."

Gus Sztorc said, "That's part of the problem."

Lonnie said, "Yeah, well, spare me the sermon."

"Spare this," Gus Sztorc said.

Lonnie sat back. He looked at the storm. They hadn't called it this big, this intense. All this snow, blankets of it, coming down thick and sticking. Plows banging down the turnpike, sanders scattering sand like fertilizer on a lawn. If he left for the theater now, he'd miss the first facial, maybe the next, depending on how well the plows were working out east.

"We better roll," Lonnie said.

"*Adios*," Gus Sztorc said, standing.

"But Gus, we okay here?"

Gus Sztorc said, "Sure."

Lonnie said, "I talk to Jimmy, give you a shout at home, yeah?"

Gus Sztorc said, "After the dirty movie?"

Lonigan shrugged. "A man's gotta do what a man's gotta do."

Gus Sztorc said, "Don't make a mess."

Lonigan got the tab, and they walked out together.

"How's Lisa," Lonnie asked.

Gus Sztorc said, "How's Lisa? Her bedroom is pink, and she scrapes the cheese off pizza, that's how's Lisa."

Lonnie shook his head. "How'd two guys like us, marry two broads like them, you ever wonder that?"

Gus Sztorc took his friend's hand. "Not too much anymore."

Lonnie said, "I hear you."

He watched his friend scrape an inch of snow from his windshield. He watched the Monte Carlo recede into the slow traffic on Jericho, then he went back inside to the phone by the men's room. He was feeling a little guilty, but he was starting to get the beginnings of something that felt like an idea.

"Yeah, meet me at the mall," he said into the receiver.

"The mall," he said, "the mall—what are there, a half dozen? The fucking mall, over by Macy's. Half an hour."

He hated talking to his brother-in-law like that, but what could he do? Gus Sztorc was right. The guy was an asshole. An asshole that hated Gus Sztorc.

In the men's room he took a leak, one palm flat on the wall. You shake it more than three times, you're jerking off. He heard that when he was, what, twelve? Thirteen? Right around the time he met his wife. And Jackie Capello. He shook it more than three times. "I'll show him a putz," he muttered.

The ride home, he kept the wipers and defrost on high, and still the windshield looked like it had been smeared with Unguetine. He felt as blind as his poodle. Plows and sanders—modified garbage trucks—pounding all over the place. Snow covered the sand a minute after it spread. Every ten yards an accident. Even four-wheel-drive pick-ups abandoned. Some of them already snowed under. He wondered if the woman's body was snowed under as well. He wondered if he should have waited with her, should have called the cops . . . But this was manslaughter, plain and simple, no matter how you looked at it. He hadn't intended to kill, but he had intended to deceive, to expose, to embarrass, and the chain of events his garbage instigated led directly to the woman's body splayed out in the snow. He wondered if anyone found her. Someone would have to have found her. But what if they didn't? What if she got plowed? Gus Sztorc shuddered. He almost wanted to puke.

The radio was no help—just news about the storm and a lot of the bullshit songs that were hits after Sinatra and before the Beatles. The only music he liked was the Italian love songs. Jerry Vale, there was a singer. The rest of these clowns . . .

Clowns made him think about Lonigan, wasting his retirement in the dirty movies, not that Gus Sztorc had the answer. He slept past noon, walked dogs, and gift-wrapped garbage. Not exactly a breakthrough. But at least it was something, a worldview. Lonigan, day after day, with his beer or his whiskey and his dumb Danish broads with the New Jersey accents. Once he passed out in his seat. The manager threatened to call an EMS.

Still, Lonigan wasn't always a clown. He was crazy brave, and crazy strong. They almost had to issue him a new chest for all his medals in Korea. He was loyal, and he was a goer. He'd fly at a man twice his size, Gus Sztorc had seen him do it. And it didn't take much to make him fly. One cross look, one dumb remark. He'd been in four fights just since retirement, and he lost only one, to his ex-wife. He'd missed a support payment, and she found him at the dirty movies. She hit him with her wedding ring right in the orbital bone. Hairline fracture blackened his eye damn near two weeks. Looked like he was wearing a hockey puck for a monocle. He had to squint to see the skins.

Lisa Sztorc sat in the kitchen reading editorials in Suffolk Life.

"You got a call from someone," she said. She slid a note on the table his way.

"Who?"

"Your friend from the mall, he said."

"My friend from the mall?"

"That's what he said."

"I don't have any friend from the mall," Gus Sztorc said. "What mall?"

He punched in the number he didn't recognize.

"Hello, asshole," a man's voice said.

Gus Sztorc said, "Who's this?"

"No," the voice said. "Who are you?"

Gus Sztorc pulled the phone from his ear. He looked at the receiver. Something about the voice was . . . peculiar.

"If this is a joke," he said, "I'm not laughing."

"No one's laughing on this end either, motherfucker."

"Hey, there's a woman in this room, you son of a bitch. If I knew who you were I'd smack you in your goddamn mouth."

"You want to know who this is?" the voice said. "This is the guy whose wife picked up what you dropped at the mall."

"The mall?"

"Ah, we're gonna play games now? The mall, asshole, where the blood is still wet in the snow."

"You must have—"

"Okay, so we play games," the voice said, and the line went dead.

Slowly, Gus Sztorc set the phone back in the cradle. He stared at the side of the refrigerator with the calendar. For months, every day was blank. The kitchen was yellow. The refrigerator was yellow. You open the fridge, the Saran Wrap is yellow. He fought for his country so his wife could match the Saran Wrap to the wallpaper. So his kids could become pukes.

He grabbed the leashes hanging off the front door knob and his dogs jumped up.

Every car that passed him on his walk to the beach scared him shitless. With the snow, it was like they were driving on cotton—he couldn't hear them until they were right at his back. And how could they see him? He could hardly see the dogs at the end of the leash. Any one of the cars, he thought, could be the caller. And any one could strike him, run his fat ass over, and who could ever accuse the driver of negligence?

It made perfect sense, when he thought about it. He always expected a bum deal. In this life, you don't get even laughs free. And if you live honest—a simple life full of sacrifice, climbing poles all winter with your fingers numb so your wife can drive a Volvo and your sons can study poetry in college— you deserve what you get. He had nothing but disgust for his life, and resigned dread for his future. He was almost better off back at work. At least there he had guys he could talk to about how there was nothing to talk about.

At the beach, he unleashed the dogs and they charged down to the shoreline. How did they even know the way? He started walking blind, and every now and then one of them raced by, the wind lifting their fur. He should have helped the hurt woman. Lonnie was right—what was he afraid of? But it was the whole horror of it—the utter nonsense of the fight over a booby prize, and then the sound, the dull thunk of her skull catching the Buick's rear bumper, like a foul ball pinging off the pole of a backstop. How in the hell, he kept wondering, did someone know it was him? Was it the woman in the car? Did she make his plates? If she made his plates, how did she track them?

When he'd had enough of the cold and the wind and the paranoia, he turned back toward the parking lot. His eyes were half frozen. He whistled for the dogs. Only the schnauzer appeared. He called and whistled after the other. But she'd done this before. She was getting older, she was less enthused about challenging walks in the weather. More than once she'd turned around, slipped past him, found her way back home alone.

The garage was empty. He thought, I don't even get dinner in a snowstorm.

On the stove, a can of Campbell's Chunky—beef and country vegetables—sat inside a small pot with dark burn marks across its bottom. On the top of the can was a Post-it. "Don't forget to add water. The boys are out with friends. Your friend called again."

He threw the note, the can, and the pot in the garbage. He crumpled two slices of Kraft's individually wrapped American cheese together in each fist and dropped them in each dog's bowls.

"Don't eat your sister's," he told the schnauzer.

The schnauzer ignored him. She went straight to the poodle's bowl and cleaned it out, then she cleaned out her own.

Gus Sztorc slid out the side door.

At Bernie's on Sound Avenue, a pair of young couples hugged each end of the shuffleboard table. The guys and the gals wore flannel shirts and jeans. Gus Sztorc was glad he wasn't a young man now. The way they dressed, how did they know who was who, which was which. And when they figured it out, what would it matter.

He ordered a boilermaker, threw back the whiskey and sipped the beer. Then he ordered another. "The boys are out with friends," he thought. What the hell did he care? What the hell did they care? Another phony Christmas. This year they gave him a robe. It had the hotel's name on the pocket. A pair of pukes. Did they think he was that stupid?

The news was on. On his second beer, the incident at the mall appeared—a woman in the parking lot, found dead from injuries sustained from a fall. Anyone with information could call this number. Gus Sztorc took change from the bar and entered the phone booth.

He dialed Lonigan while watching one of the flannel shirted gals lean over the shuffleboard, her ass like twin halves of a large cantaloupe. Maybe it wasn't such a bad time to be a young man after all.

Lonigan picked up on the second ring. "You watching the news?" Lonigan asked him.

"I thought you was at the dirty movie," Gus Sztorc said.

"I went to the mall," Lonigan said. "See what I could see. A buddy of mine's in trouble."

Gus Sztorc said, "Semper fi."

Lonigan said, "You got that right."

"So what did you see?"

"A couple of cops eating doughnuts behind yellow tape, you know, the usual."

"You know 'em?"

"I know all the cops."

"And?"

"And nothing. They think the broad slipped by accident. The bumper she hit was her own. They scraped some hair and skin and blood off it, but no one suspects shit."

Gus Sztorc said, "Not no one."

He told Lonigan about the call his wife took, about the conversation he'd had with the caller, about the new note.

Lonigan went bat shit. The kind of this-is-what-we-fought-for obscenity-laced rant they threw when things got grim. In the background, he could hear Lonigan throwing things, breaking things, stomping on their broken pieces.

Gus Sztorc said, "For Christ's sake, Lonnie, stop. You wreck anybody's house, make it the caller's."

And hearing that, hearing the caller referred to as "the caller," set him off again. Gus Sztorc made a mental note to take him to Sears when this was all over, help him pick up some new shit.

When he'd calmed down a bit, Lonigan said, "You know what you do? You set up a meet."

"Set up a meet?"

"Call his ass back, ask what he wants, and set up a meet."

"And then what?"

"Then I show up and break his goddamn nose."

"What if," Gus Sztorc said, but his friend was already off the line.

He bought a round for the girl with the cantaloupe ass and her friends and took his change. He drove home in second.

His low beams swept across the front yard. Scattered across the snow were the contents of the package he'd left at the mall. He idled the Monte Carlo and kept the headlights on the mess. Sinking to his knees in the snow, he grabbed at the debris. There it all was again, the paper and wrappers and pie tins. He carried it with both arms to the garage where he dumped it into a large refuse bag.

That's when he saw the poodle, on its back, four paws in the air, rigid. Its head had been twisted completely around. The schnauzer crept over to Gus Sztorc's boots and nuzzled. Gus Sztorc picked her up. He lightly scratched her belly while staring at the belly of his dead dog.

He stuffed the dead dog into a grocery bag and hid her body behind a row of hemlocks in the backyard. He'd bury her when the ground thawed. Then he called his friend from the mall.

"Hey, we missed you, big guy."

"You won't miss me again," Gus Sztorc said.

"Ooo," the man said. "That's the way—uh-huh, uh-huh—I like it, uh-huh, uh-huh."

"What do you need me to bring, asshole?"

"Uh-huh, uh-huh," the man sang again.

The morning was cold and quiet. Nothing in the harbor stirred. Way off at the breakwater, the fresh white snout of the Port Jefferson-Bridgeport ferry pushed into the calm harbor, its horn a flat *wonk, wonk, wonk*. The docks and the boats in their moorings were heavy with snow. Everything seemed dulled, arrested, killing time. Pylons looked like they were wearing hats.

From a second-story deck of Danford's Hotel, Lonnie Lonigan swept the marina parking area with a cheap pair of field glasses, the kind that pop out of a wallet-sized packet.

"I can't see a fucking thing with these," he said. "This is what they give you on the force?"

His brother-in-law, Jimmy, the cop, said, "Fix the focus. You gotta fix the focus."

"I did fix the focus."

"You can't see the ferry?" Jimmy asked.

"Of course I can see the ferry," Lonnie said. "Of course I can see the ferry. The ferry's big. We're not looking for big things, are we?"

"I'm just saying," Jimmy said. "Let me see."

He took the glasses from his brother-in-law. Lonnie was more like his older brother—fourteen years separated Lonnie from his sister, Jimmy's wife. Sometimes he acted like Jimmy's father. Lonnie had walked his sister down the aisle, and the one time Jimmy got caught cheating on her, Lonnie broke his nose. Gus Sztorc held his arms, and Lonnie broke his nose. He never forgot it.

Jimmy peered into the parking lot with little satisfaction. "They worked okay in Vegas."

"You brought these to Vegas?"

Jimmy said, "Fucking A I brought 'em. I wanted to see everything up close."

"How much closer can you get to a hand of cards?" Lonnie said.

"Not for the tables, the shows, the shows."

"You saw shows?"

"Sure I saw shows. They got shows everywhere."

"What kind of shows?"

"Everything, Lonnie, I told you."

"Tell me again."

Jimmy's shoulders slumped. "Is this some kind of test?"

"I'm interested," Lonnie said. "I'm just asking."

"You're never just asking."

"So what do they got?"

"And you're never interested."

"Come on, Jimmy, tell me. I can't stay at the porn show the entire time."

"You will."

"But if I don't—what do they got?"

Jimmy shook his head.

"You know. They got tigers, white tigers . . . everything."

Lonnie said, "You're an idiot." He grabbed the glasses. "There's only one kind of show I'm interested in."

"Yeah, well I don't know about that," Jimmy said. "I was with Meg."

Lonnie said, "Goddamn right."

Jimmy said, "Come on, gimme a break."

Lonnie said, "I'll give you another break."

"You know," Jimmy said. He stopped himself.

Lonnie asked him what.

"Nothing."

"No," Lonnie said, "what? I want to hear this—are you fronting off?"

"I'm a goddamn cop, Lonnie, you know—you should show a little respect."

Lonnie said, "Respect this."

Jimmy pointed to the parking area's entrance.

"There he is," he said.

"There's who?"

"Your friend."

"I don't see shit," Lonnie said.

Jimmy pulled the field glasses from his eyes. There, in the distance, was Gus Sztorc's Monte Carlo, smoke puffing from its exhaust.

Lonnie said, "Right on time."

Jimmy said, "You sure he don't know who's calling?"

Lonnie said, "Gus? He don't know shit."

"He's smarter than he looks," Jimmy said.

"You're smarter than you look," Lonnie said. "What's that tell you?"

Jimmy muttered something else about being a cop.

"Quit whining and get ready to move."

"Does he got the package?"

"We'll know when he parks and gets out, won't we?"

Gus Sztorc rolled to a stop at the pair of orange traffic cones that reserved a parking space. The car next to the reserved space, a Plymouth Gran Fury, was just like the voice had described it: a cream colored four-door sedan with cardboard bent and folded over the license plates. He put the Monte Carlo in park, got out and moved the cones, got back into the driver's seat and pulled alongside the Plymouth and cut the engine. From the terrace on Danford's third floor, Lonnie Lonigan could see the gray-white puffs of exhaust sputter and die. He and Jimmy backed into their room and peered through the blinds.

Gus Sztorc got out of his car. He went to the passenger side and opened its door, wide, and stepped aside. He counted to ten, then he pulled the seat forward and stepped aside again. This, he assumed, was in order to indicate to whoever was watching that no one was in the car with him. He counted to ten again. Then he opened the trunk, stepped aside, counted. He got back inside his car, his heart pounding.

On the seat alongside him was a shoebox, wrapped in Christmas paper, a big red bow in the middle. He'd followed instructions exactly, exactly how his "friend from the mall" told him. He'd gone to the bank, he'd withdrawn five thousand dollars—almost every nickel in his account—and he'd stacked it in the box, using newspaper to fill up the open space. Now, he waited, his eyes fixed straight ahead at the ferry. It seemed almost still in the water, or as if the shore went to meet it rather than it pulling in. But there it was, a few more loud blats on the horn, and into its mooring it bumped.

The grinding sound of metal engaging metal raised Gus Sztorc's shoulders to his ears. The wide mouth of the ferry opened slowly, slowly, slowly, down toward the algae green-and-brown concrete ramp.

Three sharp taps on the Monte Carlo's trunk startled him. He looked up and saw a hooded man walk briskly past. When the man had reached the docks, Gus Sztorc got out of his car with the box. He didn't look anywhere but at the ground. He approached the hood of the parked Plymouth, placed the shoebox just behind the ornament, and returned to his car. He started up, backed out, and gave three toots on the horn.

"Good boy," Lonnie said. "And my apologies to the Mrs."

Lonnie watched Gus Sztorc for as long as he could see the Monte Carlo, down the length of the parking area, in line with the half-dozen or so cars that had disembarked the ferry, and then right onto Main Street heading toward Setauket.

Then he noticed the punk—a greasy little punk with hacked-up hair and jeans painted-on tight. He was standing at the Plymouth's hood, looking this way, looking that. He started pulling at the box's bow.

Lonnie burst out onto the Danford's deck.

"Hey," he shouted.

The kid looked up and ran.

He ran like a gazelle.

Lonnie ran, too. He ran like a hippo. Three car lengths he was sucking air so hard it burned. Four, he doubled over, clutching at his left arm, coughing from his throat into his colon. He tried to call out to Jimmy, but he couldn't get his breath. The kid hit the docks, his feet flying, before Lonnie hit the pavement.

Jimmy started walking back toward the lot when he heard Gus Sztorc honk. He walked slowly, the hood pulled tight around his face. He wanted this to work perfect, he wanted to pay Gus Sztorc back, even if it wouldn't get him a nickel. By the time he saw the kid, and what the kid carried, the kid's Converse sneakers were already slapping the dock.

"Hey," he shouted. "Police."

The kid threw a shoulder into Jimmy's chest and sent him flying onto the deck of a moored cruiser. The snow broke Jimmy's fall, but the thud took the wind out of his lungs. The kid swung onto the ferry, and took a staircase up to the passenger deck.

That's when Gus Sztorc returned in the Monte Carlo. He took the same spot and he leashed up his schnauzer. He walked her over to the fallen man face down in the snow. Several people had gathered around.

"Shouldn't he be face up," Gus Sztorc asked.

One of the onlookers said he didn't have a pulse.

"Oh," Gus Sztorc said. "You're a doctor?"

He continued to the dock, where he advised the dockmaster to call an EMS.

Jimmy brushed snow off the ladder that led to the cruiser he'd landed on. Carefully, he pulled himself up one slow, slippery step at a time. Something had gone out in his back, it hurt him to reach, and it hurt him to step. Probably at least a busted rib, maybe two.

"Oh, hello officer," Gus Sztorc said. "Do you need a hand?"

He stood where the ladder reached the dock, his desert boots even with Jimmy's face. He planted the right boot in Jimmy's teeth and sent him flying back down on the deck. The schnauzer peered over the edge and barked at Jimmy's prostrate form.

Gus Sztorc said, "Happy holidays."

He turned and boarded the ferry. It felt colder than he'd expected. Suddenly, the idea of taking a ride on the water seemed a bit unnecessary, if not absurd. But it's what his son had insisted—his price for helping out—and he climbed the steps to the passenger deck to find him. That might not be as easy as it sounded. His son wouldn't be the only greasy little punk with hacked-up hair and the jeans painted-on tight.

TRAVEL

The summer before I started college, I took a job at Magellan Travel, a small travel agency on New York City's Upper West Side. The owner, Sebastian Siegel, was a friend of the Kennedy family. The office manager, Libby Morendo, had been romantically involved with one of The Kennedy clan. She was twenty-six, perpetually tan, having always just returned from somewhere, and her eyes were the kind of aquamarine that travel magazines use for cover shots of the Caribbean.

Libby had traveled all over Europe, some of Asia, even Africa—that while she was dating the Kennedy. Theirs had been a passionate affair, covered in the tabloids, cheered by the public: the prince of America's royal family, and the Brooklyn girl, daughter of a man who owned a bakery. The Kennedy had introduced her to the world, Libby introduced him to the cannoli. We read about them trekking the desert, ranging across the savanna, documenting the game preserves, in articles including Libby's photographs of The Kennedy handling venomous puff adders and huge-beaked birds of prey.

One thing The Kennedy couldn't handle was his mother, whose disapproval of Libby finally broke them apart. Not long after their break-up, The Kennedy suffered a near fatal heroin overdose and was photographed on a stretcher carried from a commercial airliner. Upon recovery, he purchased Libby an apartment in a brownstone near the Museum of Natural History, a block and a half from Magellan Travel, and he instructed his friend, Magellan's owner, to hire Libby as office manager and special travel consultant to the Kennedys.

And that summer I met them all. Coming, going, planning, hanging around.

"John needs a four-wheeler in Quito," I'd be informed.

"Chris will return via Madrid, not Rome."

"Add a tenth seat to the Oaxaca booking."

Flocks of Kennedy boys dropped down from their aeries and balconies, and Siegel opened folding chairs for them on Columbus Avenue outside the office. With the collars of their polo shirts turned up, they drank Heineken from green bottles and shouted to the chic, lithe women who'd pass by—the "schools of fish," Siegel called them—"Yo, snapper." Before cracking a second beer, they'd start reeling them in and Siegel would re-enter the shop.

"Libby," he'd say, pointing at me. "I need to borrow the boy."

Siegel would have me re-fold and re-closet the chairs, then direct me to the bodega for more Heineken, which I was instructed to deliver, quietly, to Siegel's brownstone right off the park. Often the living room and terrace would be vacant. I'd linger, then, and listen to the sounds of sex, all of which emanated from the women, the Kennedy boys oddly silent, I thought, for all that talk about their legendary testosterone. Sometimes I'd pop myself a Heineken and tiptoe around the digs, thinking, so this is how a friend of the Kennedys lives. Shards of champagne flutes lining the fireplace, tightly tubed hundred-dollar bills on the coffee table, the walls a checkerboard of framed photographs, many of them half-familiar: Kennedys and their friends smiling on the sides of mountains, on sailing yachts, in attendance at the houses of state. When I looked at these photographs, I'd picture the aquamarine pools of Libby's eyes, their wistful, distant look which, I believe, provided my first lesson in real politics.

Back at Magellan, Libby would look at me from behind their pools, as if to ask, "Was he there?" Once, so heartbroken for her, I returned with a bouquet of freesia and irises. Libby rose from her seat beaming. "Are these from . . . ?" she said, then melted back into her seat, the gloom once again falling over her eyes. She fell silent and mirthless for the rest of that afternoon, even when I called her line direct and played the Marlboro theme on the phone buttons.

I traveled that summer, too, back and forth on the Long Island Rail Road between Magellan Travel and my parents' home on Long Island. When I'd get home, my mother would ask, "Who came into to the shop today," hoping I might have had a glimpse of the imperial Jackie O.

"She lives across the park, Mom," I'd explain.

Next in the hierarchy of Kennedy possibles were Jackie O.'s children.

"They live on vacation in airplanes, Mom."

Third was Senator Ted.

"He shuttles between Washington and Hyannis, Mom."

"I thought you said you see them all," she'd say.

And I'd say, "I do, but we're not allowed to talk about it."

"Oh," she'd say, "so you did see Jackie?"

"Jackie lives across the park, Mom."

"You're impossible," she'd say.

"The job has rules," I'd tell her. And I'd tell her that the Kennedys were just like you and me, "Only worse," I'd say.

"Only nobody wants to know about you and me," she'd say.

"Does anyone want to know about Libby Morendo?" I'd say.

Libby came from the same forlorn neighborhood as my mother, yet she'd attracted the attentions of a Kennedy.

"How is Libby?" she'd ask.

And I'd say, "How do you think?"

"Right," my mother would say. "It's hard enough getting over an ordinary person. But a Kennedy . . ."

In order to facilitate my helping out at Magellan, Siegel put me up at various Kennedy or Kennedy friend apartments while their owners skipped the globe. I walked their dogs, fed their fish, watered their plants. And in one case, the case this story concerns, I moved a car from one side of the street to the opposite.

"A Kennedy parks on the street?" I said.

Siegel frowned, then pretended he hadn't heard. We were not supposed to betray, on any level, that we had any awareness whatever of the identities of these privileged personages whose peregrinations made all our jobs possible.

I was disappointed to discover that the Kennedy friend's car was a BMW. One of those sober, classy things of little or no aesthetic value and with perhaps a third of the pep of the cars I still secretly admired—the Firebird, the Road Runner, the GTO.

The BMW, and the apartment, belonged to someone whose last name was not Kennedy. On his mailbox though, appeared the name X Kennedy X, the same name that appeared on all his mail. His shirts, the majority of them, were monogrammed and the letter "K" was their monograms' most prominent feature. If he'd had a choice, he would have called himself Kennedy Kennedy Kennedy—KKK for short, and that's what I came to call him.

Moving the BMW to alternate sides of KKK's street was easy enough, although it made me late for work twice a week. Of course, Libby couldn't complain. It must have been doubly troubling for her to know that KKK was traveling with The Kennedy, her Kennedy, first class, of course, from New York to Costa Rica, Costa Rica to the Galapagos, the Galapagos to Venezuela, and from there to Brazil.

One day, I came in an hour late.

"The parking," I explained.

I placed a fresh coffee on Libby's desk and took my own.

"Nice shirt," Libby said. "Is that new?"

I had "borrowed" one of KKK's shirts, soft black cotton with two pockets, made in Italy. He had the same shirt in olive, earth, and gray. For some reason, he'd neglected to monogram this model. "This?" I said. "Not really."

"You haven't worn it before," she said.

Actually, I had, just not to work.

"It's KKK's," I admitted.

Libby said, "Don't call him that."

I said, "Give me six reasons why not."

"Because Sebastian will fire you if he hears."

"That's one."

"He's a nice guy."

"Nice guy," I said. "That's not what I hear."

"What?" she said. "You mean those stories?"

"I think they're more than stories, Libby. I mean all those girls can't be lying."

She shook her head. "They used to say that about . . ." Her thought trailed off, and her eyes blanked into the middle distance. This happened several times a day. You could be talking about the beaches on Tobago or the possibility of tourism in space, and the jukebox of Libby's brain would skip right back to that scratched up and over-played single, the sad one I wanted desperately to rescue her from.

I realigned a display of brochures on luxury train travel in Andalusia. I imagined my thumbs pressing into The Kennedy's esophagus. "Wake up, you privileged fuck," I'd shout, shaking him by the throat. "Wake the fuck up."

Two other women worked in the office. Angela Calabrese, twenty-five years old from Queens, was pretty in that gum-cracking outer borough "Leader of the Pack" kind of way. Her tan was of the scorched brown variety, acquired from hours with her skin smeared in baby oil at Rockaway Beach. Around her waist she wore narrow gold belts, and her shoulders were broad and uncovered and tan-lineless.

And there was Noelle Starr, twenty-eight, a Julliard graduate, a dancer whose dancing days ended after a series of worsening injuries. Noelle was delicate. She complained about air conditioning and secondary smoke and for lunch she nibbled grapefruit wedges and four-ounce cartons of non-fat cottage cheese.

All they ever talked about was men. They talked as if I wasn't even there. How bad the men were, how desperate they themselves were. And that amazed me.

"Do you have any idea," I'd tell them, "how beautiful you all are?"

Noelle would say, "You're sweet."

Libby would say, "For what that's worth in this town."

And Angela would say, "You're a boy, of course we're beautiful. You think we're all your mother."

And she would lean on my desk and allow her blouse to

fall open, revealing the soft tan globes of her b-cup breasts, perfectly taut little Sunkist oranges that made my cheeks red and my tongue soft and my loins warm and thick.

"See?" she'd say. "A real man would grab me by the neck and kiss the lips right off my face, or he'd ignore me. But you," she said, snickering and straightening her blouse, "you get all bent out of shape, like your mommy's about to bring you your scooter pie."

"Aww," Noelle would say. "Leave him be."

I'd say, "It's okay."

And Libby would say, "Of course it's okay. If the worst thing that happens to you here is you get flashed by Angela, I'd say that's a pretty good summer job."

And I'd say, "I'd rather get flashed by you."

"Aww," Noelle would say.

And Libby would redden.

"Really," I'd insist, but I knew that wasn't true.

I was learning something about myself that summer, something that caused me more than a little concern. Libby was soft, sad, and ethereal, and my fantasies about her ran a kind of vanilla rescue gamut. I would pull her from rough surf, then comfort her on the beach at sunset. I would remove my jacket and cover her head in a downpour. I would threaten to break the arm of the guy who deceived her. These scenarios warmed my heart, and I mean deeply. There were times when I wanted to take her soft cheeks between my hands, look into those soft shimmering blue-green pools, and kiss her soft lips softly and for a very long and very soft time. The fantasies never involved nudity, or sex, despite the fact that Libby was by any standards a lovely and sexy woman.

Angela, though: about her I never had a pure thought. The

most frequent fantasy involved Angela nude except for a gold waist-belt and a pair of mules. She is bent over a desk, propped on an arm, one mule on the floor, the other up on the desk blotter, and with her free hand she offers me a sniff of her index and middle fingers which she has just removed from her ass. Her pussy is as hairless as a vanilla wafer. On the raised leg, a floss-thin gold ankle bracelet hangs slack below a band of untanned skin. I could never picture dining with Angela, or strolling hand in hand, or curling on a sofa, and my fantasies were devoid of conversation that didn't directly pertain to her body parts or their smell. Still, she owned my dick—even though in my heart I had awarded that appendage to Libby.

Early most Mondays, sunburned and carrying a small valise, Siegel slid into Magellan and dropped car keys on my desk.

"The red Mustang," he'd say, pointing to the avenue. "Get it back by three." Then he'd stagger out, crippled from a summer weekend debauchery.

Hertz was over on 48th and 10th. After lunch, I'd cruise the blocks between 10th and 11th, some of them lined with idling buses, some of them dotted with parked cars, their exhausts shimmering. Streetwalkers worked this stretch as naked as they could appear in public without risking arrest. Some wore fishnet danskins and stiletto pumps. Some wore leopard-print brassieres and micro-minis. They smiled, waved, flagged down, the big black ones gamboling up to cars, their exposed flesh jiggling like pudding against cellophane.

The streetwalker I liked was a bit different. White, blonde, svelte, and pushing thirty. She called herself Sandy. Her get-up was classic noir: a trench coat, dark glasses, little else. She didn't chase after cars, she approached only those that idled and waited for her to summon the initiative to push off her length of wall. Real style. You got the feeling she was more interested in reading the books that sometimes stuck out from her jacket pockets.

"Going out?" Sandy'd ask.

I'd hold up my hands in the gesture of "broke."

"I don't charge a night at the Plaza, honey," she'd say, and I'd pop the lock. Sliding in, she'd say, "How much you got?" She'd run her fingers over the Mustang's new upholstery. "Car like this, you can't be too broke."

As though I was just now checking, I'd dig through my pockets and arithmetic whatever came up in my hands.

"Seven thirty-five," I'd say, feigning disappointment, "and one token. Is that enough?"

Sandy gazed through the windshield. The broken land-scape—its sparse traffic, its leveled lots surrounded by link fences dotted with brown bags and Styrofoam trays, its other girls smoking in the heat or pressing cleavage into the open windows of parked cars—helped her calculate.

"Well," she'd say, "I am out of tokens."

And I'd smile.

"But that's not gonna get you much."

"I don't need a lot."

"Okay then, baby, so what do you need?"

Shrugging, I'd say, "I don't know."

"Mama knows, though, doesn't she?"

"I guess."

"Yeah," she'd say, leaning down, undoing my belt. "Mama knows so fucking good."

When I returned from one of these sessions, Angela was so much easier to handle.

"You like these?" she'd say, bending forward at the copy machine.

I'd look at her real cool. "They're okay," I'd say. "I give them a B, B minus."

Noelle and Libby would laugh, and Angela would straighten.

"Listen to Joe College here," she'd say. "B minus. And he hasn't even matriculated."

That summer, my relationship with my father thawed. What that meant, pretty much, was that now he didn't ask me to mow the lawn or clean the gutters or sweep out the garage. He'd just mope around the yard with a puss on, doing it all by himself until I came out and volunteered and suddenly that intractable puss disappeared.

"Remember these?" he'd say, running his hands over a clipped hedge of hemlocks. "We planted them, they weren't two feet high."

"Yeah," I'd say, "and now they're not even three."

"Height," he said, "is not the point."

And I said, "Evidently."

"Look," he said, bending down to the hedge. "See?"

I bent down and looked where he looked.

"See what?" I said. "All I see is green."

He stood up, satisfied. "That's what I'm talking about. That wall of green, you couldn't see through that with a telescope."

"So?"

"So?" he said. "So privacy, so."

I said, "Yeah, sure, Dad, for dachshunds and dwarves. You'd have to duck down three feet to get the privacy."

"You gotta have patience, Cliffy. You can't make a hedge grow faster than a hedge grows."

True enough, I thought, but if you really needed to conceal yourself from observation, there were quicker, more efficient ways.

Things were okay with my mother, too. I'd given up trying to rescue her from my father, since from his docility it appeared she'd won.

She continued to ask about the Kennedys, and I continued to tell her that they weren't very good people.

"Are they better than the Nixons?" she said.

I said, "High standards indeed. Look what he did to Libby," I reminded her.

"The mother did that to Libby," she said, "and didn't he nearly kill himself? Didn't he buy her a brownstone?"

"An apartment *in* a brownstone," I corrected her.

She said, "You know what I mean."

I said, "So if I do something awful to a girl, I can blame my mother?"

"Don't call your mother *your mother*," my father said.

My mother said, "You did something awful to a girl?"

"He better not," my father said.

I liked to be in New York on Saturday nights. At ten, I'd walk over to the bookstore on Broadway and finger through the titles I would soon be reading for college. And by eleven, I had the Sunday *New York Times*.

A block or two north in the West 80s, some of the Tenth Avenue hookers appeared and lingered. They leaned against the glass at bus stops, smoking and pretending to be waiting for the 104. Taxi drivers picked them up and, ten minutes later, dropped them back off in the same spot. The hookers would exit heavily, chewing fresh gum, and like autumn leaves gum wrappers fell from their brittle fingers and gathered at the corners of the bus shelters.

One night a police patrol car slowed, and the hookers dug in their purses for change.

"You lost?" the young cop said, rolling down his window.

"Where the phone at?" a chunky black hooker in a yellow wig answered.

"You need to make a call?" the cop said. "You get one free at the precinct."

"Funny," the hooker said.

"Right," the cop said, tapping his wristwatch. "I'll be back in ten. Don't make it sad, you hear me?"

Another night I spotted Sandy.

"Come here often?" I said.

Sandy smiled. "I will now," she said.

She threw her cigarette to the sidewalk. She took my arm in hers and we walked toward the park.

"Seven thirty-five and a token?" I said.

Sandy said, "No way on Saturday night, babe."

"Well," I said, trying to think what else I could offer.

She fingered the edges of my Sunday Times. "Seven thirty-five, a token, and the *Book Review*."

"Are you serious?" I said.

Sandy said, "As a judge."

I pinched out the *Book Review*. "How about *Help Wanted*?"

Sandy gave me a look.

"Where we going?" I asked her.

She led me to a set of steps leading under the front porch of a brownstone. It wasn't until she was kneeling and I was in her mouth that I realized the brownstone we were under was the brownstone in which Libby Morendo lived.

"What's the matter, baby?" Sandy said, looking up and gently feathering my balls. "I'm already unexciting?"

I shook my head. "I know someone who lives here."

"Oops," said Sandy. "A girl?"

I nodded, picturing the sadness in Libby's eyes, the defeat in Libby's posture.

"So pretend I'm her," Sandy said. "Call me her name."

Simple problem, simple solution.

I cupped Sandy's head and put a little English on my thrusts. "Angela," I said, "Angela."

That Monday Libby called in sick.

"You want me to bring you anything?" I asked.

"Put Angela on," she told me.

When Angela hung up, I said, "What's the matter with her?"

Angela said, "What do you think?"

"Not The Kennedy," I said. "He's halfway up the Amazon."

On Angela's desk was an open copy of *People* Magazine. She spun it around and pointed to a color layout. It featured The Kennedy on tour, the same kind of spread Libby used to document with her Leica. There he was in the Galapagos walking past giant tortoises hand in hand with a naturalist identified as Dr. Melanie Fein. The caption read, "Beauty and the Beast." Dr. Melanie Fein wore cuffed khaki short-shorts and a khaki bush shirt knotted at the center of her perfect abdominals. An Amazon shot captioned "Someone to Lean On" featured Dr. Fein in a bikini, leaning over the railing of a skiff. And on Copacabana Beach, above the caption "When in Rio," The Kennedy thumbs-upped the camera while pointing to Dr. Fein's buttocks, fully exposed in the Brazilian-style floss-bikini.

"Wow," I told Angela. "She looks just like you."

Angela said, "She looks like a frikking tramp."

"This one in Rio," I said. "What cheek."

"Not funny," Angela said.

"No," Noelle said, "funny. Inappropriate, but funny."

"This family has no shame," Angela said.

"Wait," I said, "it's not The Kennedy's fault."

"Oh shut up, you young fuck," Angela said.

I said, "Maybe they met on the Galapagos, fell in love, you know. He can't help people taking pictures of them."

Noelle got up and riffled through Libby's files. She opened a folder on my desk to a letter from The Kennedy. It read, "Please include a full-itinerary booking for Dr. Mel Fein, family physician."

I said, "Oh."

Later, Siegel slumped in, pinching the bridge of his nose between thumb and forefinger.

He pointed outside. "The uh," he said, "the uh . . ."

"I know," I said, "the Mustang by three."

He dropped the keys.

"Where's Morendo?"

Angela glared at him.

"In bed for a week," she said.

"For a week?" Siegel said, tossing me a wink. "What, she meet someone?"

Angela flung the magazine at him. She said, "Page forty-six."

Siegel looked at Angela, then at the magazine on the floor, then me.

"Could, uh—"

"I'm not picking it up," I told him.

"Jesus," Siegel said, "what is going on here today?"

He bent for the *People*. "Christ I need a coffee."

No one moved.

He said, "I'll get it, I'll get it." He riffled through the magazine's pages. "You said what page?"

No one spoke. Siegel shook his head, and then he found the spread. "Hey," he said, "it's [The Kennedy]."

He sat down.

"Ai-yai-yai, Dr. Fein," he said, "I need a full cavity exam!"

He made several additional comments, all of which I agreed with in fact if not in spirit. Angela chewed the erasers off pencils. Noelle blew over the surface of her tea.

"Okay," he said, "so?"

"So?" Angela said. "You figure it out."

"This is what upset her?"

Angela said, "Duh."

"They split up almost two years ago."

Angela said, "Three."

"So what is her problem? For Christ's sake, she had some fun, she traveled the world, and she got a job and a brownstone out of it."

"An apartment *in* a brownstone," I said.

"You know what I mean," Siegel said. "And who asked you?"

"She's not a whore," Noelle said. "You don't just use someone and buy their feelings, brownstone or no."

Siegel shook his head and smiled incredulously, as if we were all dense. "No one said *she's a whore*," Siegel said, his hands measuring out the clause. "What I'm saying, *he's a Kennedy*. When is that finally going to register with you people?"

"So he's a Kennedy," Noelle said. "What does that mean?"

"What does that mean?" Siegel said. "What are you, twelve?"

"What does it mean?" I said.

"It means," Siegel said, "the rules don't apply to them—they're the *Kennedys*."

For lunch, I drove Siegel's Mustang rental over to KKK's place. I went through his drawers and closets, and I loaded two suitcases and a pillowcase with items I felt would help with my imminent matriculation and ensuing liberal education: a boxed set of Puccini operas, a cycle of Mahler Symphonies, *The Basic Writings of Sigmund Freud*. I packed the four un-monogrammed shirts, a Guatemalan *campesino* tunic, and a Scuba-Pro half-inch exposure suit with a CO_2 powered speargun.

The phone was ringing when I came back for the second bag.

I said, "Yeah?"

"Who is this?" the voice said. It appeared to be coming over long distance.

"No," I said, "who's *this*?"

The voice identified itself as The Kennedy.

I said, "No shit."

"Every time I call Magellan," he said, "someone cuts me off."

"And you got a problem with that?"

There was a silence.

"Who is this?" he said.

"This is the guy," I told him, "who's telling you, and probably for the first time, that you're a prick."

The Kennedy laughed. "The first time today?" he said.

I said, "Whatever."

He said, "I guess that makes you not a prick."

Now I was silent.

"I guess you're a good guy, right? Always does the right thing, the audiences erupt in applause?"

"How could you do that to Libby?" I said. "She's the most lovely and vulnerable woman I've met."

We talked for half an hour. By the time I hung up, I felt like I was the villain, the guy was that smooth.

"Let me ask you something," he'd said. He said, "When you close your eyes, and you got your paws clamped over your pecker, whose face is it you see on your dick? I mean in your mind's eye?"

"Just get to the point," I told him.

"Do you see Libby, that lovely and vulnerable woman, or do you see Angela?"

I fell silent again. "Well," I said.

"That's my point," The Kennedy said. "I was lying to myself. To my dick. You ever lie to your dick?"

I didn't respond.

"Right," he said. "Me too. Libby is a beautiful woman, but she's not the kind of woman who can own your dick, at least not mine. And at some point in your life you have to take responsibility for the truth of your erections, and not the bullshit in your mind, and what that bullshit convinces your heart. You follow me?"

"I'm getting the drift," I told him, "even if I don't want to."

"The only difference," he said, "between you and me, or maybe I should say between me and most men, since I don't know you and maybe you are the one really decent guy, whatever that means, but the only difference is that I can do pretty much what every guy dreams of doing, and I can get away with it. The price is everybody knows, or they find out eventually. I mean, they publish pictures."

I knew there was something wrong about his thinking, something twisted and self-exonerating and falsely accurate.

But there was something irrefutably right about it, too, and I wound up feeling like: Who am I to argue with this guy? He's The Kennedy.

"So," I told him after a while, "what do you need?"

I took down the notes for his new itinerary with Dr. Fein, KKK, and now a Brazilian heiress whose family owned hotels. They'd be dropping down further south. Tierra del Fuego, then Cape Town, then the Seychelles, from where he'd call again with new details.

"But listen," he said. "When I get back, lunch and drinks, okay?"

"Sure," I said.

"No, I mean it," he said. "On me."

Back downstairs, I emptied the trunk of the Mustang of its contraband. I left the cases packed on KKK's bed, give him something to think about when he got home.

At Magellan, I left The Kennedy's new itinerary on Noelle's desk. I knew she'd handle it.

I dropped the Mustang at Hertz then walked over to 48th. I couldn't see Sandy anywhere, although a half-dozen other girls loitered with intent.

"Anyone seen Sandy?" I asked.

The girls all exchanged looks.

"I'm Sandy," said a thick waisted black woman in leopard underwear and high heels.

"I'm Sandy, too," said a skinny Latina in a micro-mini and purple fishnets.

I said, "The Sandy I'm looking for has blond hair, wears a trench coat, sunglasses."

"The writer?" the Latina said. "She finished her book."

"Writer?" I said. "Book?"

"But maybe I can give you a hand . . ."

My mother and father picked me up at the railroad station.

"You look exhausted," she said.

I shrugged. "Life in the city," I told her, getting into the backseat.

"What is it," my father said. "You excited about college? You think you're gonna come out smarter than your old man?"

My mother said, "He reads the syllabus he'll be smarter."

He gave her a look, but he dropped the discussion.

At the exit, he turned north for the scenic backroads.

"You're taking the backroads?" she said.

He shook his head and turned for the main highway.

If you asked me, my mother owned my father's dick, but maybe not in the way that The Kennedy had meant. Or maybe it was my father's balls she owned. Maybe when we met for drinks The Kennedy could explain the difference, if there was one.

On the main highway, my mother said, "So who came into the shop today?"

"Marilyn Monroe."

"No, come on. Who did you see?"

"Lee Harvey Oswald."

"You don't want to talk," she said, "don't talk. I'll play the radio."

She reached for the radio.

"Don't play the radio."

"Then who did you see?"

"JFK."

She reached for the radio.

"All right," I said, "all right."

She kept her hand on the on/off button. "Well?"

"I didn't see jack, or Jackie, but I did have a long conversation."

"Who with?"

"You ready?"

"Come on, who?"

And I said the name of The Kennedy.

She lit up. "The [The Kennedy]?"

"The same," I said. "Know what he told me?"

"What?"

"He said I'm just like him."

"No, really," she said, "what?"

"I'm telling you," I told her. "He wants to meet for drinks."

She turned on the radio. Apparently, someone had left a cake out in the rain.

"Don't believe me," I said.

"He said that?" my father asked, the makings of a smile tugging at his lips. In the rearview mirror, he caught my eye. "He said you're just like him?"

I said, "Don't believe him."

THE PAULA AND CLIFF FRAGMENTS

Paula and Cliff do Netflix

Paula says she doesn't want *Raging Bull*. She doesn't want horror or westerns, can't stand *noir*. She reminds Cliff about the course in cinema she'd signed up for in college with her best friend, Mary Chris, how the course began with Hitchcock's *The Birds*.

"*The*-fucking-*Birds*," Paula says. "I looked at Mary Chris like, these people are speaking *English*!"

Paula wanted subtitles, she wanted ideas, she wanted Eisensteinian montage.

"I wanted films," Paula says, "that questioned the existence of God."

Cliff says, "*Noir* questions the existence of God."

Paula says, "Then *reaffirms* it."

"Ah," Cliff says, "so a John Ford western."

They settle on a documentary about figure skaters.

Paula and Cliff at Ray's Pizza

Paula is scraping the cheese from her slice of cheese pizza.

"What are you doing," Cliff says.

Paula says, "What does it look like I'm doing?"

Cliff says, "It looks like you're scraping the cheese off a slice of cheese pizza."

"Bingo," Paula says. She bites into the white dough wet with pink sauce.

Cliff says, "Well, why are you scraping the cheese off a slice of cheese pizza?"

"*Because*," Paula sings, "*the world is round, it turns me on.*"

"Ah," Cliff says, "so something does."

Paula stops mid-bite. "If you're referring to what's happened since I started Zoloft . . ."

"What?" Cliff says. "Something happened?"

Paula says, "You're such an asshole."

Cliff burps, wipes his mouth, gets up.

"Another slice?" he says.

Paula and Cliff in Bed

Paula says, "Open your eyes."

She says, "Talk to me. Tell me what you want to do.

"To me," she says, "what you want to do to me.

"Say my name, say it in my ear, but with passion. Passion!

"Spank me," she says. "No, like you mean it. I've been a bad girl. A very bad girl.

"I fucking love you," she says, "you know that, don't you? You should fucking know that."

Paula asks, "Why do you love my cunt?

"And don't say *pussy*, I hate that fucking word."

"Don't say *cunt* either," Paula says, "unless it's my cunt you're fucking. Is it my cunt you're fucking?" Paula says.

"Baby?

"Tell me," she says. "Tell me in my ear. Tell me louder. Tell me like you can hardly talk."

Paula and Cliff at Mary Chris's Gallery Opening

Cliff stands in a corner where two blank walls meet. On the walls opposite, peculiar work hangs, work that makes Cliff feel vaguely uncomfortable.

Paula says, "You haven't even looked at her work."

Cliff tells her no, actually, he has.

And he has. On at least two occasions, one quite recent, he and Paula visited Mary Chris's studio, and Cliff had looked at her . . . work. To Cliff, it resembled dirty socks dangling from finishing nails on strips of 1x4 plywood. Perhaps because it was dirty socks, according to Mary Chris and according to the plaques alongside each "piece," dangling from finishing nails on strips of 1x4 plywood.

"I mean tonight," Paula says. "You haven't looked at her work tonight."

Cliff says, "You know it makes me uncomfortable."

Paula says, "It's supposed to make you uncomfortable."

"Then I'm not doing anything wrong," Cliff says.

"You could make an effort," Paula says.

Cliff supposes that, yes, he could. "But as you say, I'm feeling the right way without making any effort at all."

Paula shakes her head. She says, "Sometimes . . ."

Cliff says, "Unquestionably."

Paula and Cliff at Couples Therapy

Paula isn't talking. "There's nothing more to say," she says. "There's nothing more to add, I've said it all a thousand times—nothing gets through, nothing matters. I'd talk if it mattered, if it did any goddamn good."

The counselor suggests that this kind of talk isn't hopeful.

Cliff disagrees. He says that Paula not talking is hopeful, it's the most hopeful thing he's heard since they started therapy. He'd never miss another session if he knew Paula wasn't talking.

Sarcasm, too, the counselor says is unhopeful.

Cliff says, "What sarcasm?"

Perhaps, the counselor suggests, they might consider unhopefulness as a bridge. Not a chasm they have to shout across, but a bridge that actually links them. All they have to do, he says, is start walking toward each other, step by step by step.

Paula is the first to snicker.

Cliff snickers, too.

Then they laugh. They laugh till they cry. They fill tissues. Then they're at time.

THIS IS NOT HAPPENING TO YOU

You are now in the proximity of Extra-Strength Tylenol caplets. Don't trust your shaking hands, bend to the kitchen counter, dip to the spilled caplets like a dog to a puddle. Tongue several up, a half-dozen, never mind the recommended dosage. At this point, to consider recommended dosages would be a category mistake. Recommended dosages apply to children or adults and you, you remember head-poundingly, belong to neither category. You are a headache, an extra-strength headache, nothing more. Focus, do not multi-task, be here now.

The fridge, the half-quart of Old Milwaukee, crack it . . . and linger briefly in that reassuring *skershsh*, the audio anesthetic of it, the promise of its wet sizzle. Lift the can, tilt back your head, and pour the lager heavily over your tongue and onto your sawdust-dry throat. Feel the caplets pebble past the uvula, scraping the parched ringlets of the esophagus, hear them "plip" into that vast vat of Saturday night stewing in your guts on top of Friday's vat, Thursday's vat, the vats of your weeks and months and lifetimes in New Orleans. The Old Milwaukee chills your sternum, its crisp cold bubbles ping wetly in your skull. Slowly it stills your trembling fingers until they hang from your wrists inert as gloves. In your eyes gather pools of relief.

With relief begins perspective. Rather than unpuzzling the night, better to consider where you just were, only minutes before the Tylenol accomplishment: the dining room floor amidst overturned furniture and scattered Tylenol caplets.

Many good people have been found on floors: William Holden, Lenny Bruce, Janis Joplin. Good company, all, and isn't Sunday a day for company?

Company requires food. On the kitchen counter, an avocado, or what remains of it. How quaint: you—or someone—had taken pains to militate against hunger, a condition that would arise only in the future. Evidence that some level of maturity's been achieved. You are not hungry now, at this very moment, but this object, this avocado, it intrigues, it calls to you. On inspection you discover that one side of this avocado is grooved, its green skin gouged, its soft yellow flesh ridged. Ridged, you speculate, by what appears to be a pair of teeth not your own. A rodent's teeth? You measure the groove against a book of matches. It is a wide groove, matchbook wide. You are not an orthodontist, not an oral surgeon, nor have you earned any graduate credits in zoology. Still, you feel qualified to venture a second speculation: this groove was not made by the teeth of a mouse, or Bugs Bunny. Find the flashlight. Is it under the sink? Poking about, banging into objects, you imagine rat teeth sinking into your knuckles. Forget the flashlight, light a match. Light two matches. Now poke past the insecticide canisters and find a rat trap. The rat trap made with glue. Many French Quarter rentals come replete with rat traps. Peel open carefully, set the trap glue face up (not like the last time) where the avocado had been, there where a patina of rat fur subtle as tooth plaque laminates the formica. Set it snugly against the formica ledge, but allow the crack between ledge and counter to breathe. In order for the trap to succeed, everything around the trap's milieu must appear normal, so you must provide passage to your housemates the cockroaches, who will press up through the crack onto the ledge and scitter-scatter across the rat trap, leaving at least their scent, perhaps the coffee-ground speckles of their droppings, and these reassuring signs will encourage the rat to venture into the sticky shallow La Brea of his destiny. You are thinking like a rat, cautiously, selfishly, and horizontally sniffing out possibilities in front of your bloodshot beady eyes. Satisfied, you can anticipate results.

Now: you have worked. You have arisen to find a problem in your home, two problems—your head, the avocado—you have addressed them, and they have been dispatched, with prejudice: a thirst has been raised. This thirst creeps up from your stomach and down from your lips, two separate thirst-fronts creeping, creeping, creeping like desert sand in steady wind until they join at the throat and provide a satisfying discomfort—satisfying in that this fresh discomfort introduces a new challenge, a challenge you now meet with the new Old Milwaukee you are cracking. Oh, that stinging in the throat, that dry desert sand washing back whence it came, cool oases irrigating your eyes. *Ahhhhhh*, you think, the poetry of *ahhh-hhh. So very fucking ahhhhhh*. You are confronting problems. You are meeting them on the playing field of life and the problems are trailing, nil to three.

Like life, you find Sunday, too, is a problem and you have constructed strategies to address it. On the surface, one might find your strategies formless, shapeless, random. But isn't that precisely the point? Form is emptiness, emptiness form. *Bodhi swaha!* On Sunday one awakens to problems one can count on—blue laws, headaches, the crossword puzzle; and problems particular to each specific calendar occurrence of Sunday—today's grooved avocado comes to mind. In this sense, Sunday is both a comfort and a challenge. A character is defined, you recall reading, by its struggles with challenge.

Now there is the challenge of your hunger, a vestigial drive at this point, a habit more than an urgency, but there is strength in ritual, comfort in repetition, meaning in tradition. What tradition might you employ then against your hunger?

The avocado.

Inspect the avocado. Can you salvage the ungrooved portion? Can you cut the groove out from the soft ripe yellow flesh, excavate it in a sense, then scrape your own choppers against the flesh's green shell? You can't see why not, can you, and you're the only one looking (unless, unaware, you are observed by the rat or its minions). So ask yourself: should you be reluctant to place your teeth near where the rat dragged his?

All god's chilluns gots teeth, you're thinking, *even Mr. Rat.*

And don't you hear the rats each night, gnawing their teeth clean on the rafters in your attic? Wouldn't dirty teeth fail to leave clean grooves?

Convinced of the viability of said avocado, you look for a clean spoon, a clean knife, anything to avoid actual contact with the remnants of Mr. Rat's spittle. A bit squeamish, perhaps, but you don't know Mr. Rat personally, you don't know his habits with floss. With spoon in hand, look for the dish soap. Failing that, look for a scrub. Where might a scrub be? Ask yourself, and be honest, are you really that hungry?

Reschedule the avocado.

Wash down more Tylenol.

Engage the outdoors.

Up Dauphine Street, paw through the late afternoon humidity, a humidity that hangs like a shower curtain.

Ah, Vieux Carré, you talk a lot, let's have a look at you. Think I busted a button on me trousers, hope they don't fall down.

On the sidewalk the hymn of flies on redolent dog drop-pings baking in the sun with a metallic aromaticity. Consider the regularity of said dogs, the solidity of their stools, the satis-factions the dogs must anticipate every time they assume their pinched posture. Try to recall the last solid stool you passed. Is it your bipedality, you wonder, or your booze that prevents you from experiencing the pleasure of that most canine release?

Avoid the carcasses of roaches the size of harmonicas. Avoid carcasses.

Approaching the corner of Dauphine and Touro, you discern the sickening deposits of last night's bacchanal per-colating throatwards. Clutching the sticky trunk of a banana tree, you hurl. Violently, agonizingly, remedially. Even as you discharge, you think. You are thinking, you are a thought machine. It's a juxtaposition this time that commands your ideation, the juxtaposition "pink-green vomit and brown-black Louisiana loam." You are not certain if "loam" is the correct term, horticulturally speaking. You are not certain if horticulture is the correct term. You are certain that you don't give a fuck because although your gastro-intestinal distress has been somewhat alleviated by the reverse peristalsis, your head now hurts worse. *A bit of a pain in the Gulliver* . . . And there in the pink-green, brown-black gloop of yester-eve you spy the barely dissolved, barely discolored Extra-Strength Tylenol caplets, the very things that enabled this excursion. Two con-flicting impulses obtain: disgust at the puke and the objects of relief that lie therein.

Some persons, you reflect, many even—that vast horde of unstout souls, might, at this time, experience the first stirrings of remorse, depression, self-recrimination. Not you. This is not happening to you, it is happening to the Undiscovered

Genius, the character you've created to play you in the tragi-comic farce you know as "your life." The talents of this Undiscovered Genius have yet to manifest in any recognizable form that might ultimately be remunerated by an institution, a governing body, a critical faculty, a network or publishing house, or rewarded by an adoring public. Its nebulosity, you understand, is part of its genius: the suspense! What form will it finally take, you imagine the public you have yet to seduce wondering? As far as forms are concerned, you have already conceded painting; painting is a form for which you demonstrated little if any aptitude. This was evidenced early on and most acutely by the F you took, and deserved, in ninth-grade Studio Art, the year you gave painting the brush. Singing, dancing, the violin . . . these, too, have been purged from your schema. You are practicing the process of discovery through elimination, one step at a time.

Baby steps, increments, walk before you run. These are the building blocks of emotional maturity, psychological wellbeing, if not wisdom. You are, for the moment, satisfied, undissuaded. You retrieve the Tylenol caplets. Demurely, you palm the caplets along your shorts, then mouth them. And you take comfort in the fact that there is nothing that hasn't been seen in New Orleans, nothing that hasn't been done. You proceed, head held high, the caplets dissolving, toward the avenue.

At the Li'l General, the beer is buried in the back. Grab two forties. Rip a bag of pork rinds from the wire rack. Rip another. Pinch some hot sauce from a shelf, deliver it to the transvestite who works the register. Do not acknowledge her wink. Do not acknowledge the privileged glimpse she affords you of her newly acquired and, objectively speaking and all context removed, perfectly lovely cleavage, cleavage that, you must admit, sometimes has you imagining improper intimacies. Do not acknowledge the warm stirrings of your loins. You are a man, you come from an era before sex drives became gendered norms. You have no norms. You are instinct. Instinct with boundaries, and this realization carries you back to your earlier speculations re: maturity, psychological well-being, wisdom.

With a look of concern, she says, "Sugar Pie, are you going under?"

You tell her a man's gotta have breakfast.

"It's suppertime, Sugar," she says, ringing you up, her long nails clacking on the register's keys. "Besides, pork rinds and hot sauce do not a breakfast make."

Technically, you tell her, it's brunch.

Ignore her offer of brunch.

The *New York Times* is stacked by the door. Grab one.

On Esplanade, you field strip the paper. The News, the Region, the Week in Review, Business—they all join the beer cans and go-cups and chewed ears of corn bulging from the wire mesh trash basket. Garbage you are happy to leave behind.

Ah but time will tell just who has fell, and who's been left behind . . .

The rest awaits your scorn at home.

On the avenue's median, a bearded man walks two giant schnauzers in the shade of the sycamores. This would be you, you reflect, if you had a beard. *You, If you Had a Beard*, you think: there is a title. You, if you had two schnauzers, you if you had a life. You if there were living things whose welfare depended on you.

The leaves of the banana trees hang like wet towels over the heads of the frail humans who pass below in the fogs of their own biographies. Slow traffic idles by as if it's arriving from the 1950s. You have arrived from the late 1960s by way of the Reagan '80s. A life bracketed at one end by Question Mark and the Mysterians, Debbie Gibson at the other. Your once reckless idealism slowly turned to cynicism and that, you can't for the life of you remember when, turned into despair. Despair was the last feeling-state you recall inhabiting. You recall it, like your long-lost evacuations, with a certain physiological nostalgia. Now you are a drunk, and the feeling-range that that lifestyle affords is either: working well, or not working well. When it's not working well, its failures are the issue. When it is working well, there are no issues. And isn't that a reasonable definition of freedom? Not that you're a particular advocate of reason. Or freedom, for that matter. You may have been once, one, or the other, or both, since, in your thinking they don't appear to be mutually exclusive. But these are Sunday afternoon ideations under the sagging banana trees of the Vieux Carré, two years into Reagan's second term, a tickertape of monkey-mind nonsense, really, something to occupy the restless coconut on your shoulders while you step around dog droppings and over the thick roots pressing up sidewalks.

On Frenchmen St., the pedestrian traffic lingers before pottery shops and thrift shops and schedules for bands at Snug Harbor. On a lamppost, the announcement of a new play: *I Found a Brain Inside My Boyfriend's Head.* Check the name of the playwright—do you know her? Have you balled her? Balling—that other vestigial drive. A woman is just a woman, you're thinking, but an ale, a cold ale, even a warm flat stagnant ale, an ale with a fly floating in its scuzz, an ale torpedoed by cigarette butts, an ale impossible to distinguish in color and general rancidity from the urinal in Coop's, that ale can save your life, and has.

You start at the Arts & Leisure, and the groans begin. That should have been you in the "Conversation with the Filmmaker," you in the "Profile: Up and Coming"—if you had had the connections. Just look at the names: Redgrave, Coppola, Lennon . . . does anyone start out on their own anymore? Who the fuck did, like, Adam know, back in the garden? Fucking Yawveh?

Sauce up a pork rind, swallow some ale, turn the page.

Move on to the Book Review.

The groans resume.

That should have been you doing the review. No: you being reviewed, you creeping up the "New & Noteworthy," responding to earnest questions with transcendent irony. If you hadn't been stuck in a public school. If you hadn't quit the public school. If your parents read books instead of watched television. Toss the Book Review, toss Arts & Leisure, toss them the fuck across the floor to . . . ah, yes, the TV.

Surf the narrow range of TV channels. A gospel show, an evangelical event, local news figures chatting, a couple of Cajuns fishing, reruns of reruns. You mute the box and stand in front of your record collection, that vast catalogue of the best of mankind. What music do you *need* to hear? What *gnossiènne*, what ètude, what Concerto in H-moll will create the correct adjustment to the afternoon's numbing malaise? But now you discern another noise . . .

. . . a scraping . . . from the direction of the kitchen . . . *et voila*!

Monsieur Rat (suddenly, you hope momentarily, he has become French), asquirm upon his bed of glue, pinned from the narrow underbite all the way to the asshole. Only the tail and one rear leg, working furiously, remain unstuck.

He is long, slender, gray. Obviously guilty. Still, you interrogate indirectly.

"So tell me," you begin, "you like avocados?"

The rat wriggles with a violence that vibrates the trap, its fear rippling from ass over ribs.

You wonder at its slender physique. Wouldn't the meat of an avocado, with its generous fat content and abundance of carbohydrates, wouldn't it flesh out a little rodent, fill in the valleys between the ribs?

"Maybe you're the wrong rat?" you say, and the rat just wriggles. "Still," you suggest, "you wouldn't be in a fix like this if you hadn't done something wrong, sometime somewhere. Am I right?"

You turn on the faucet, and the sound of the water rushing further animates the rat's anxiety.

"Relax," you tell it. "You're not guilty, you won't drown. How do you like it, warm? Hot? Cold?"

With a broomstick you nudge the rat closer to the sink. Its contractions become more violent.

You watch the sink fill. It is dirty. It will be dirtier. Make a note to move before it needs to be cleaned.

"What do you think?" you ask the rat. "You ready? Meet this shit head-on, get it over with?"

The rat's spasms cause the trap to bounce slightly along the formica.

"Ah come on," you say with exasperation, "work with me on this."

Now it is shitting.

It continues to shit when it hits the water, a dirty ink the color of charcoal trailing out its ass like a streamer from a party favor.

"Hey," you tell it, comfortingly, "you gotta go, you gotta go."

You watch it struggle, watch it wrestle its fur from the glue—a shoulder, maybe a leg—but as soon as one part's free another is stuck. You place the broom handle at the trap's corner and press the trap under. The struggle slows, becomes smaller. Spasms, shudders, tiny bubbles. No disrespect intended, but a measure or two of Don Ho cross the endless jukebox of your mind.

"Aloha," you tell it.

Et voila—Monsieur Rat est mort.

You look at it there below the surface, its sharp tiny teeth, its long black whiskers, its innocent eyes, and damn if that's not a grimace of horror you see on its face.

Suddenly there's a part of you that's not so glib. You can feel it, there, just under your ribs. A kind of mammalian identification, a kind of dread, a kind of premonition. But in the same instant that you feel it, it disappears. Poof! Gone. It's not happening to you.

You grab your hat, the crossword puzzle, a pen.

"Be cool," you tell Mr. Rat.

You're ready to go out

JUST TELL ME WHO IT WAS

Cliff waited until the commercial to hit mute, then he asked his mother a question that had been on his mind, to one degree or another, for some twenty-five years.

"Who were you talking to that day?" he said.

His mother looked up from the *Newsday*.

"What day?" She tilted her head back slightly and looked over the rims of her glasses.

"You know," Cliff said, "back when you initiated your policy."

"My *policy*?"

"Your telephone policy."

She looked at him blankly. "I don't know what you're talking about."

"The telephone policy," Cliff said. "Remember? The one where it didn't matter which one of us bothered you on the phone, we were both punished."

She shook her head. "Come on," she said impatiently, pointing at the TV, "the news is back on."

"Fuck the news," Cliff said. "I'm talking about the time you came careening into my room with your loafer drawn."

"My loafer drawn?"

"Swinging your goddamn loafer until you broke my elbow."

Cliff's mother recoiled. "You're nuts," she said.

"Needed a cast halfway down my ribs," Cliff said, his hands at the sides of his ribcage.

She flipped a page of the *Newsday*. "You made more sense when you were drunk," she said.

"Good answer," Cliff said. "Supportive answer."

Slowly she dragged a finger down a column of print. It was clear to Cliff that, under his scrutiny, she wasn't able to read a word.

He said, "Tell me what you just read."

"Will you leave me alone?" she said.

"Just answer the question," Cliff said.

"What question?"

"Who you were talking to. Who could have been so important as to be worth breaking my fucking arm?"

"Now it's your arm."

"Elbow."

"You sure it wasn't your head?"

"It certainly could have been," Cliff said. "It would have been if I hadn't raised my arms." He showed her how he had raised his arms. "Remember? Arms over head, peeking out between hands to see where the next blow was coming from? The way me and Wally had to walk around you. And him," he said, thrusting his jaw at a photograph alongside the TV. In the photograph his father, dead now five months, shook hands with Mario Cuomo, his expression a mixture of humility and awe. "Look at him," Cliff said, "like he's ready to goddamn genuflect."

His mother said, "You know, you're beginning to get on my nerves."

"Yeah?" Cliff said. "What are you gonna do, break my other arm?"

"Maybe I should," his mother said.

Cliff said, "The two of you, beating up on children. If Cuomo only knew, right? Or do you think he broke his children's bones, too?"

His mother removed her glasses. "Is this what you talk about with your shrink?"

"Just tell me who it was."

"I bet you have her completely snowed. 'Oh, they hit me. Oh, they abused me.' Not, 'Oh, I been on drugs twenty-five years and leeched every nickel I could.'"

"You don't want to say who it was," Cliff said, "or you can't remember?"

"Boy, I'd love to get into one of those bullshit sessions," she said. "I'd straighten her right out."

Cliff said, "That's an idea—you can attend a session!"

She said, "I might as well, I'm paying for them."

"Then would you tell *her* who it was?"

She laughed.

"Right," Cliff said, "big joke. Body cast. Funny."

"I don't know what the hell you're talking about."

"What were you gonna do next, run us over with the car? That would have been a real riot, right? Full traction, a pair of fucking mummies in intensive care."

"That's what you got right here at home," she said, "you and your brother. Intensive care."

"So what's the big secret then," Cliff said, "if you feel so secure in your parenting? Just tell me who it was."

"Who what was?" she said, her voice rising. "Who what was?"

Calmly Cliff said, "Who were you talking to, that was so fucking important, on the day that Wally started something that interrupted your conversation but instead of punishing him, you made me, completely blameless, the first victim of your new policy?"

Cliff was getting to her, he could tell. Her cheeks had

colored pinkly, and the skins of what might be tears appeared to press up from her eyes.

Cliff continued. "I'm not saying you came in with the intention of breaking my elbow. But you came in swinging, didn't you? Swinging and screaming. Not listening, not thinking, on full throttle, weren't you? Just luxuriating in that rage, like you weren't leaving until you'd done some damage."

"Let me ask you a question," Cliff's mother said.

Cliff ignored her.

"What did Dr. Holman tell you," he said, "when he took you into his office, huh? That you were some miserable fucking child beater, was that it? That you were one step from getting sent away to fucking jail where you belonged?"

"Let me ask you something," Cliff's mother said.

"We're talking about you now, not me."

"What were you doing all those years," she said, "when we sent you to school?"

"You didn't send me anywhere, I got in on my own. Full scholarship."

"Scholarship my ass," she said. "Then what was all that money for? Your liver? What did you do, drink up every goddamn penny your father and I ever sent you, you're supposed to be studying so hard?"

"He didn't send me shit," Cliff said. "He didn't even talk to me."

"Don't kid yourself," Cliff's mother said. "He sent you. He sent you loads. He was proud of you."

"So," Cliff said, "you're saying you broke my elbow when I was what, seven? Eight? Because you intuited that someday, when I was twenty-something I'd wind up drinking too much in college?"

"You drank too much in junior fucking high."

"So you admit you broke my elbow?"

"I don't want to talk about it."

"But you remember it now? The event of it."

"I remember you had some casts, yes."

"*Had some casts*," Cliff repeated, as if the words caused a funny taste in his mouth. "*Had some casts*. I love it," Cliff said. "That's brilliant. *Had some casts*. Like a collection, like I collected them."

"You didn't have casts?" she said. "Isn't that what you're saying, you had casts?"

Cliff shook his head.

"This is insane," Cliff said. "I can't have this conversation."

"We're not having it," she said. "At least I'm not."

She picked up her glasses. They were wide, large-framed, and boxy with garishly decorated temples.

Cliff continued to stare at her.

"I can put these back on now, right?" she said.

"You're fucking amazing," Cliff said.

"What?" she said. "We agreed we're not talking about it, right?"

He picked up the remote and un-muted the TV.

"The news is over," he said.

She shrugged. "I have the paper."

"What channel you want?"

"You're not gonna watch anything?"

He shook his head.

"What channel?"

"Put it on thirteen."

He pushed back in his chair.

"You don't want tea?" she asked.

"Later," he told her.

He grabbed a section of the paper. When he reached the doorway, she spoke.

"It was your father," she said.

Cliff paused. "I thought so," he said. "How come?"

She said, "It isn't rocket science."

"He was seeing someone?" Cliff asked.

"Again," she said.

"Wow," Cliff said. "Maybe I will have some tea."

She pushed back from the table. He sank back into his chair.

"You want regular," she said, from the cabinet, "or de-caf?"

"Regular." Cliff said. He watched her pull out the mugs, a Democratic National Convention 1980 mug, at which she'd been a delegate, and a Columbia University mug, at which Cliff had been a student.

"You should have let him," Cliff said.

"Let him what?" she said.

She filled a glass kettle with water and set it on the stove. It was hard to believe, Cliff thought, that this small-framed woman with the pale skin, the hips wider than the shoulders, and the soft protrusion of belly, could ever have contained so much violence.

"See someone," Cliff said.

She said, "Oh really?"

"Things were a lot nicer when he wasn't around," Cliff said. "Weren't they?"

She stood alongside the stove waiting for the water to boil.

She said, "That's not the way we did it back then."

"No," Cliff said, "you just broke elbows."

"Stop saying I broke your elbow, okay. Stop saying I broke your elbow."

"All right," Cliff said. "You didn't break my elbow."

"Thank you."

"But can you tell me who it was?"

"I just told you."

"No, I mean who he was seeing."

She said, "What?"

"Tell me who Dad was seeing."

"You're some piece of work," she said.

She set a mug of tea at his place at the table.

"Who was it?"

She said, "Go ahead."

"Go ahead what?"

"Go ahead and say I broke your elbow."

She brought a hot mug to her place at the table and sat down. She folded the first section of the newspaper, opened the second.

"Come on," Cliff said, "Just tell me who it was."

REUNION

The boy could never forget how his German shepherd Wolf loved the woods, and he often went for walks in the woods alone, remembering those times he'd let Wolf get ahead of him, way ahead of him. And when he thought Wolf was far enough ahead, and completely engrossed in tracking down some scent, the boy would ditch into a thicket to hide, sometimes he'd climb a tree. And Wolf would come galloping back, frantic, whimpering, sniffing, barking, searching the terrain. And then, on finding the boy, he'd wriggle from neck to tail and cover the boy's face with licks as if he hadn't seen him in weeks. And the walks would resume, at first with caution, with Wolf only steps ahead, checking back frequently, more concerned with the boy behind him than he was with the smorgasbord of opportunities ahead. Until, little by little, the scents pulled him farther away, step by step, yard by yard, and once again the boy would spot the chance to trick the dog, which he did, and the separations and reunions would repeat, over and over, all day long, day after day, with licks and laughter and love.

But one day Wolf pulled away for good. He bit his third paperboy, on the property, in the driveway. Knocked him down, got his mouth around the paperboy's waist, from bellybutton to spine. The boy's father saw it all. "He could have bit that kid in two," his father said. The neighbors lined the street, glowering, their arms folded at their chests. There was no other choice, the boy's father explained. They'd have to get rid of the dog. "To a good place," his father promised. But his decision was final. "Tell him goodbye tonight," his father said. "Tomorrow he goes."

Both the boy and his father cried when Wolf hopped up on the passenger seat. The boy's father backed out the driveway, and the boy chased them down the block, past the glaring neighbors, and all the way out to the turn on to 25A. Wolf barked, but the boy couldn't hear him. His wet black nose streaked the rear window.

In the early months of Wolf's exile, the boy took some comfort in picturing the dog gallivanting across fields, leaping fences, chasing down rodents. He was placed, his father promised the boy, with a farmer who owned acres and acres of rolling hills and dense forest with winding trails you could get lost on. It was somewhere out near Yaphank, and he convinced the boy that the dog was happy, maybe even happier with all that land, all those woods. It helped the boy some, but he still felt lonely. He couldn't get the dog out of his head. He felt the dog's absence in his chest and stomach, like a great gaping hole, and he found it hard to do homework, to play ball, to do anything much but walk the old walks, climb a tree, maybe whistle, maybe call the dog's name.

One day a Suffolk County Police patrol car pulled to a stop alongside the boy. He was on his bicycle near a pond in Yaphank.

The officer rolled down his window.

"Shouldn't you be in school?" the officer asked.

The boy said he was looking for a farm.

"A farm?" the officer said.

The boy waited in the back of the patrol car—the officer parked in the lot outside the Yaphank General Post Office—until his mother came to pick him up. The officer set the bicycle carefully in the trunk of the mother's car. He secured the trunk with a bungee cord.

Another time, the boy searched the opposite direction, away from the pond. Nothing he passed looked like the farm his father had described, with rolling hills and dense forests. Everything was flat, just sod and potato fields for miles and miles. The boy pedaled so far from the pond that it got dark and he couldn't figure out which way was home. At a diner, a cashier name Rose allowed him to use the telephone. This time his father came.

"You gotta knock this off," his father told him, "do you understand?"

The boy told him that he did.

And he did, kind of. He understood, or at least he believed, that his father had lied to him. He understood that Wolf wasn't at some farm in Yaphank—he wasn't at any farm, anywhere. There weren't any rolling hills, there was no dense forest. He couldn't bring himself to ask where the dog really was, or if he was even alive. On the drive home he closed his eyes and pictured those times Wolf would find him hiding in thickets or up trees, and how every cell of the dog, from snout to tail, would shiver with delight. He didn't know how he'd be able to live long without that.

Trouble started to come easy to the boy. He became known for it; it was expected from him. He cut school and got picked up for truancy. He drank Schaefer beer and got picked up for drunk and disorderly. Once he was caught for vandalizing a model home—a fine with probation. Once he got picked up for resins in a pipe. He was charged with possession, and beat the charge on a technicality that embarrassed the police. They came after him all the more. He got picked up for hitchhiking, for violating probation, for loitering with intent. The court drew up a PINS petition—"Person In Need of Supervision"—he saw counselors and probation officers, men and women, in uniform and out.

"What is bugging you?" they kept asking him.

"I don't know," the boy shrugged. "Stupid questions?"

He heard about a pharmacy in a strip mall in Centereach. In back, the slanted doors of a basement entrance led like a ramp to an unbarred window. The pharmacy had been hit a half-dozen times—quaaludes, seconals, codeine, demerol, you name it. Kids in school spent hours with their heads on the desk, their shoulders slumped against hall lockers. The boy slipped out the backyard to 25A and stuck out his thumb.

Across the street from the pharmacy was a stand-alone 7-Eleven. The boy went in and got a Yoo-hoo and a package of Old Gold cigarettes. He pretended to make a call at a pay phone outside and kept his eye on the strip mall.

The pharmacy was on the corner. The security lights on its walls were broken. There was no light in the back that the boy could see.

A lit cigarette is like a veil. The boy fired up and crossed the turnpike. He slid in the shadows along the pharmacy wall. He took three steps up the basement entrance doors and stood at the window. He stretched an X of masking tape corner to corner across the glass panel, and put his elbow through the glass. He felt around for the lock, released it, and the window popped up an inch. He opened it halfway, muscled up, and slid in.

He had a chisel in his back pocket. He used that to pop open the door that led to the drugs. As he riffled through packages, boxes, and bottles, he heard the growling.

Around the corner slid a monster of a dog, coarse-haired

and rib skinny but tall as a greyhound with a snout full of bared teeth.

"No," the boy shouted. He threw whatever he could get his hands on—vials, bags, boxes—but the dog kept coming. And just when the dog was about to leap, the boy said, "Wait—Wolf, is that you?"

And the dog skidded across the tiles.

"Wolfie?" the boy repeated.

The dog tilted his head, he stretched his snout forward cautiously and sniffed at the boy's jeans, and then he let out a yowl. He rolled on his back, paws in the air, then sprang up. He shouldered into the boy's knees, wriggled from snout to tail, then reached up for the boy's face, licking and whimpering the whole time.

The boy dropped to the floor. He took Wolf's neck in his hands.

"Oh my god, Wolfie, what have they done to you?" he said, running his hand over the dog's ribs, and his coat, which was thinned and greasy. He felt where patches of fur had worn off the dog's hips and elbows—the dog had been sleeping on concrete or gravel. The boy felt sores and calluses on the exposed skin. And the dog was starvation thin, the kind of thin that keeps a dog mean.

"I'm taking you out of here," the boy said.

The dog wore a choke chain collar. The boy reached for a loop, when a light appeared in the hallway.

"Wolf," the boy shouted, "stay."

But Wolf had already spun, and now he was off, charging the intruder.

The intruder was an auxiliary cop from the Kraughto Guard Agency. His pistol was drawn. It flashed twice.

WHAT SHE WAS CALLING FOR

It had been nearly two years since he'd heard from Bonnie Bray, so he was somewhat surprised to hear her voice on the phone, its familiar gravel and mischief and insecurity. His voice surprised him, too: he sounded happy to hear from her. When her name came up in conversation, his recollections were harsh. But people become curiosities once you've left them behind, and it's always interesting at least to hear how they've got along.

"I'm not calling to renew our friendship," Bonnie told him.

"No," Cliff said, "of course not."

"Or anything like our relationship."

"I understand," Cliff told her. But of course he thought, "heaven forbid."

What she was calling for, she told him, was to make amends.

"Aha," Cliff said.

"Why do you say that?" she said.

"Because now I know the reason you're calling."

"But you said it like . . . I don't know, *aha!,* as if a light bulb went off and suddenly you realized a truth about me or something."

"No," Cliff assured her, "no insight achieved, no truth of any kind whatever ascertained."

A brief pause.

"Wait," she said, "why do you say *that* like that?"

"Bonnie," he said. And he heard the way he said her name. He'd told the girl he started seeing after Bonnie some of his

Bonnie stories, and the girl had said, "If I ever hear you say my name the way you say hers, we're through."

Bonnie said, "I call out of friendship and next thing I'm getting dicked around."

"No one's dicking you around, for one, and two, didn't you explicitly state that this call had nothing to do with friendship? Didn't you make that perfectly clear right at the beginning of this call?"

Bonnie said she had to get off and did. Cliff was left looking at the telephone. Then he shook his head—how familiar this feeling. The backwash of all her transgressions against him, all the slights he'd suffered, the humiliations, the infidelities, came bubbling back up his throat all day like heartburn. And over and over he heard in his mind's ear the Bob Dylan lines that formed the soundtrack of their nine-year nightmare: *I hate myself for loving you, but I'll soon get over that . . .* In bed that night he stared at his ceiling and intoned, "Heaven forbid!"

He was not surprised when two days later she called again.

"I'm sorry I hung up," she said.

Cliff said, "Not a problem."

"The phone," she explained.

Cliff said he knew.

"My sponsor said we should just agree on a date and talk then."

"A date?"

A pregnant pause ensued.

"For the amends," Bonnie said, her voice rising.

Cliff pretended he didn't recall.

"The amends, in the steps. I'm asking if I can make amends to you, Jesus *Christ*."

"Ah," Cliff said, "right. The amends. But listen, you don't have to make any apologies to me, really."

"It's not an apology."

"Whatever it is, you don't owe me."

"It's not for you, Cliff, it's for me."

"Well that's sweet of you to say, but it just underscores my point, doesn't it? It's really not—"

"Will you just let me make the fucking amends for chrissakes? I need to get this step out of the way."

Cliff paused.

"Cliff?"

"I mean, yeah, why not."

"This is why my sponsor said not to get into discussions over the phone."

"Right."

"It just brings up all this old shit."

"Indeed."

"So? Can we make a date?"

"I said yes."

"No you didn't."

"Well if I didn't I meant to, so yes, we can make a date, but I want to ask you something."

With some impatience, she said what.

"Based upon what I know of AA."

"You don't know shit about AA."

"Precisely, that's why I'm asking."

"But if anyone could use it, it's you."

"Point taken."

"Right," she said. "That's the way you always get out of looking at your own shit. Some clever remark or dismissal."

"I thought it was your shit we were going to look at."

"I can't believe you're still such a fuck."

"Whereas you've blossomed into this very different kind of a cunt, haven't you?"

The line went dead.

In his yoga class, Cliff's mind burned orange. He was the one who'd taken Bonnie to her first meeting, ACOA—Adult Children of Alcoholics. He knew she'd love it there: you could blame your parents. It was just a matter of time before she'd slide into the rest of the program, in particular AA, and once she had, once she'd begun coming back with stories about her inspirational support groups, he dropped away faster than a novice topples from headstand. She called every day for weeks, excoriating him, imploring him, even bribing him. The bribes he found particularly pathetic. *I'll do this*, she promised, *and that*. Then the calls stopped.

On the third try they almost made a plan.

"I'm just going to say a date, a time, and a place, and you can say yes or no," she said.

Cliff said, "What if the date works but the place doesn't?"

"You won't stop," she said, "will you? You will not fucking stop."

"Bonnie."

"No, fuck you."

"Thursday afternoon, four thirty, the Starbucks on Columbus and 67th."

Cliff had reservations about Starbucks but he refrained from advancing them; she already knew, if she'd ever been sober enough to listen.

Bonnie was seated in the corner window. A large grande-venti-whatever-they-call-them was on the table.

"Good to see you," Cliff said, and he meant it. Just as something had softened in him at hearing her voice, something softened at seeing her. Her frizzy helmet of hair was held back and down effectively in a bandeau. It framed her wide, round face flatteringly, an effect she hadn't often achieved while actively guzzling. He was going to ask if she was still seeing the gay chap who'd cut both their hair, but refrained. Who knew what would set her off?

"I'll just get a coffee," he told her.

"I'll get it," she said.

"Not at all," he said.

"No," she said, standing, "you're broke, I know that, and you're here as a favor to me. I'll get the fucking coffee."

"That's very considerate," he said. "*Espresso doppio.*"

He wasn't surprised that she returned with regular coffee drowned in milk. He pushed it aside. If she noticed that he didn't touch it, she didn't let on.

"I need to reiterate," she said, "this is not to be your friend."

"Understood."

"Please," she said, "just let me talk, please."

"There are two of us here, Bonnie . . ."

"Will you let me fucking talk?" she said through her teeth.

Leaning forward, Cliff felt the muscle memory of: leaning forward, lowering his voice, admonishing Bonnie. Like a broken tape loop had just been repaired.

He said, "I didn't agree to come and be talked at. I agreed to see you, to hear what you had to say."

"And you're inter-fucking-rupting me again."

"You know what," Cliff said. "Just go."

"What?"

"Just fucking go."

"What are you talking about?"

"I'm not interested in all this nonsense. Just get on with it and we can get this shit fucking *over*."

"Don't shout at me."

"Thought I ended this shit two years ago."

"*You* ended it?"

"Just shut the fuck up and talk," Cliff said.

"Right," Bonnie said, "exactly."

"Well?"

"Now I don't know where to start."

Cliff looked at his watch.

"And I can see you're really interested."

"I couldn't give a rat's ass about anything you say."

She said, "I can't believe you."

"Believe it. Look at this," he said, grabbing his container of coffee. "Goddamn dishwater." He tossed the cup at a garbage bin, hitting its side. The lid flew off, and half the coffee erupted. "I told you *espresso. Espresso! Capiche?*"

Nearby patrons moved their chairs. Several glared.

"You're embarrassing me," Bonnie said.

"I haven't even started."

"Cliff."

"Shut the fuck up."

She looked down, her eyes welling.

"You ridiculous bimbo," he said. "What are you doing here? What are you *doing* here? Half a year in AA and you're ready to what, conduct seminars? Rushing through steps like a brownie gets badges, it's disgusting. You have nothing to say to me, or to anyone. Investigate your own cesspool of puke, then you get the diploma."

They shared a cab back to her place. After the awkward love-making they'd left off eighteen months earlier, Cliff moved to go down on her.

"No, that's okay," she said, stopping him. "I won't be able."

"But I want you to," he lied.

He lay back, his head on his hands, and stared at the ceiling.

"I'm glad you came," she told him.

Cliff said he was glad he came, too.

SHANGHAI

I met a well-known English poet in Shanghai. I'd gone to hear him read at an upscale international literary festival. He seemed really out of sorts, jet-lagged and culture shocked—no one knows how to drink the way the English drink. That's where I come in. I know how to drink with all nationalities. A flag of all nations drunk, couple of territories, too.

After one or two rounds, the poet was buying.

I asked, could he explain the difference between a wanker and a tosser.

And he laughed out loud. Couldn't believe he was having this conversation in China. Ordered two more. Said this is what he and his mates talk about back in the moors. I said that made sense to me. We're compelled to figure out nonsense, aren't we? Our type, I mean. No idea why I said that. Did I mean that I, too, was a poet? Or that he, too, was a drunk?

Maybe both.

He didn't ask me to explain.

So what's the difference? I asked him.

It's a bit difficult to explain, he said, isn't it? But as near as he could figure, it's this: a tosser knows he's a tosser, whereas a wanker has no idea he's a wanker.

He said an example from the world of music might be illustrative.

[The world of music was familiar to this poet. He'd formed a rock band at university during the post-punk Thatcher-malaise. You could find one or two of their records on iTunes.

You *could*, but no one *had*, a fact that didn't really bother the poet. He was a poet, not a musician, and it was as a poet that he'd written an especially keen essay on the work of Bob Dylan, someone the poet didn't really admire much, or at least thought he didn't admire, until one day for some reason, he bought the CD reissue of *Another Side of Bob Dylan*. After a few plays, he explained, it really stuck in his craw. This was in 1987. I told him that *Another Side* had been my entry point to Dylan as well, but back when it had come out, in 1964. That surprised him. He said I must have been a year old then if I was a day. I told him I never looked my age. Got proofed at bars even after I was forty. Told him I'd seen the Beatles at Shea. That was one of the lies I told him. Don't even know why. Wonder how many he told me. Wonder if he knew why he told them.]

But back to this illustrative example from the world of music:

Shane MacGowan, he said, of the Pogues? I said yeah, I know Shane MacGowan. He said, Right, so Shane Mac-Gowan, *that* is a tosser. Whereas Bono—and he emphasized Bono in the most explicit way—Bono is a complete wanker.

We clinked the necks of our beer bottles. We were drinking Newcastles.

Important distinction, I said.

You can learn a lot about England in China.

Many stories in this collection first appeared, sometimes in slightly different form, in the following publications: "Look Closer" in *Salt River Review*, "Trap" in *Sin Fronteras*, "Before and After Science" in *Libido*, "Græy Area" in *Mulberry Fork Review*, "The Motive for Metaphor" in *Haliterature*, "This Is Not Happening to You" in *Medulla*, "Paris" in *Fast Food Fiction Delivery* (Anvil Press Philippines), "Blasphemy" in *The Gettysburg Review*, "Shadow" in *The Dirty Napkin*, "Tonight and Forever" in *Pif*, "Autumnal" in *Del Sol Review*, "Snow Job" in *Long Island Noir* (Akashic Books), "Travel" in *Milk Money*, "The Paula and Cliff Fragments" in *Unshod Quills*, "Just Tell Me Who It Was" in *riverbabble*, "What She Was Calling For" in *Tom's Voice*, "Reunion" in *Helen: A Literary Magazine*, and "Shanghai" in *Extract(s)*.

ACKNOWLEDGEMENTS

This collection is a long time coming. I owe huge debts of gratitude to all the editors who believed in these stories and gave them their first home. A particular nod to Derek Alger, editor at *Pif*, who left us way too early.

On the back cover of *Buffalo Springfield Again*, the band thanks around eighty of its influences. As a twelve-year-old kid, I appreciated that long list—it led me to musicians I hadn't heard of (Jimmy Reed), and validated my appreciation of others I was kind of closeted about (Hank Williams). I have many more than eighty, and nowhere near enough space for all, but in that spirit, for influence on language and story, and for the inspiration to carry on: *The 400 Blows*, Kim Addonizio, Eve Babitz, Jacqueline Bishop, Lenny Bruce, Syndey Byrd, Italo Calvino, Peter Cameron, Raymond Carver, John Cheever, Leonard Cohen, T. Glen Coughlin, Jacques Cousteau, Lydia Davis, Bob Dylan, Frederick Exley, *Five Easy Pieces*, Mary Gaitskill, Michael Herr, Denis Johnson, Shelia Kohler, David Mamet, *Masculin-Feminin*, Gary McCleery, Leonard Michaels, Henry Miller, Joni Mitchell, Jessen Nichols, the Nurk Twins, Augustus Stanley Owsley III, Harold Pinter, *Raging Bull*, James Salter, Ravi Shankar, Sam Shepard, Patti Smith, Susan Sontag, Robert Stone, Piri Thomas, *I Vitelloni*, Tom Waits, Edmund White, the Wild Tchoupitoulas, and Richard Yates.

And special thanks to the extraordinarily talented Mari Otsu who provided the painting that appears on this book's cover, entitled "What She Was Calling For."

ABOUT THE AUTHOR

Tim Tomlinson is a co-founder of New York Writers Workshop, and co-author of its popular craft book, *The Portable MFA in Creative Writing*. His other publications include *Yolanda: An Oral History in Verse* (Finishing Line Press), and the poetry collection, *Requiem for the Tree Fort I Set on Fire* (Winter Goose Publishing). He teaches in NYU's Global Liberal Studies program, and resides with his wife in Brooklyn, NY.